READ ME 2

A Poem for Every Day
of the Year

Also available from Macmillan

Read Me 1

A Poem for Every Day of the Year

Chosen by Gaby Morgan

MACMILLAN
CHILDREN'S BOOKS

For G.R.W.

First published 1999
by Macmillan Children's Books
a division of Macmillan Publishers Limited
25 Eccleston Place, London SW1W 9NF
Basingstoke and Oxford
www.macmillan.co.uk

Associated companies throughout the world

ISBN 0 330 39132 1 (pb)

5 7 9 8 6

A CIP catalogue record for this book is available from the British Library.

Typeset by SX Composing DTP, Rayleigh, Essex
Printed by Mackays of Chatham plc, Chatham, Kent.

Contents

January

February

March

April

May

June

July

August

September

October

November

December

January

The New Year

I am the little New Year, ho, ho!
Here I come tripping it over the snow.
Shaking my bells with a merry din –
So open your doors and let me in!

Presents I bring for each and all –
Big folks, little folks, short and tall;
Each one from me a treasure may win –
So open your doors and let me in!

Some shall have silver and some shall have gold,
Some shall have new clothes and some shall have old;
Some shall have brass and some shall have tin –
So open your doors and let me in!

Some shall have water and some shall have milk,
Some shall have satin and some shall have silk!
But each from me a present may win—
So open your doors and let me in!

Anon.

I am the Song

I am the song that sings the bird.
I am the leaf that grows the land.
I am the tide that moves the moon.
I am the stream that halts the sand.
I am the cloud that drives the storm.
I am the earth that lights the sun.
I am the fire that strikes the stone.
I am the clay that shapes the hand.
I am the word that speaks the man.

Charles Causley

The Goldfish

Through the ice swept clear of snow
There suddenly appeared a glow,

A glow of orange, then a glower,
A gaping, vacant-featured flower,

A flower which floated up, a face
Against the limits of its space,

Its space I gazed at vacantly,
As distant as eternity,

Eternity, unnumbered years
Of thought which comes then disappears,

Then disappears, a guilty wish,
As quickly as that flowery fish,

That flowery fish which turned about,
Flickered, dimmed and then went out,

January

Went out like a fading light
Into the darkness, far from sight,

From sight, but never far from mind,
Leaving its after-glow behind,

Behind, before, just once, not twice,
No second glances through the ice.

John Mole

Pleasant Sounds

The rustling of leaves under the feet in woods and under
hedges;

The crumping of cat-ice and snow down wood-rides,
narrow lanes, and every street causeway;

Rustling through a wood or rather rushing, while the wind
halloos in the oak-top like thunder;

The rustle of birds' wings startled from their nests or flying
unseen into the bushes;

The whizzing of larger birds overhead in a wood, such as
crows, puddocks, buzzards;

The trample of robins and woodlarks on the brown leaves,
and the patter of squirrels on the green moss;

The fall of an acorn on the ground, the pattering of nuts on
the hazel branches as they fall from ripeness;

The flirt of the groundlark's wing from the stubbles – how
sweet such pictures on dewy mornings, when the dew
flashes from its brown feathers!

John Clare

Minnow Minnie

May I ask you if you've noticed,
May I ask you if you've seen
My minnow Minnie
Who was swimmin'
In your Ovaltine?
For you've gone and drunk it up, dear,
And she isn't in the cup, dear,
And she's nowhere to be found, dear.
Do you think that she has drowned, dear?

Shel Silverstein

Song of the Rabbits Outside the Tavern

We who play under the pines,
We who dance in the snow
That shines blue in the light of the moon
Sometimes halt as we go,
Stand with our ears erect,
Our noses testing the air,
To gaze at the golden world
Behind the windows there.

Suns they have in a cave
And stars each on a tall white stem,
And the thought of fox or night owl
Seems never to trouble them,
They laugh and eat and are warm,
Their food seems ready at hand,
While hungry out in the cold
We little rabbits stand.

But they never dance as we dance,
They have not the speed nor the grace.
We scorn both the cat and the dog
Who lie by their fireplace.
We scorn them licking their paws,
Their eyes on an upraised spoon,
We who dance hungry and wild
Under a winter's moon.

Elizabeth Coatsworth

The Lobster-Quadrille

'Will you walk a little faster?' said a whiting to a snail,
'There's a porpoise close behind us, and he's treading on my
tail.
See how eagerly the lobsters and the turtles all advance!
They are waiting on the shingle – will you come and join the
dance?
    Will you, won't you, will you, won't you, will you join
      the dance?
    Will you, won't you, will you, won't you, won't you join
      the dance?

'You can really have no notion how delightful it will be
When they take us up and throw us, with the lobsters, out
    to sea!'
But the snail replied 'Too far, too far!' and gave a look
    askance—
Said he thanked the whiting kindly; but he would not join
    the dance.
    Would not, could not, would not, could not, would not
        join the dance.
    Would not, could not, would not, could not, could not
        join the dance.

'What matters it how far we go?' his scaly friend replied.
'There is another shore, you know, upon the other side.
The further off from England the nearer is to France –
Then turn not pale, beloved snail, but come and join the
    dance.
    Will you, won't you, will you, won't you, will you join
        the dance?
    Will you, won't you, will you, won't you, won't you join
        the dance?'

Lewis Carroll

Sing a Song of Sixpence

Sing a song of sixpence,
A pocket full of rye;
Four and twenty blackbirds,
Baked in a pie.

When the pie was opened,
The birds began to sing;
Was not that a dainty dish,
To set before the king?

The king was in his counting-house,
Counting out his money;
The queen was in the parlour,
Eating bread and honey.

The maid was in the garden,
Hanging out the clothes,
Along came a blackbird,
And snapped off her nose.

Anon.

Tony O

Over the bleak and barren snow
A voice there came a-calling;
'Where are you going to, Tony O!
Where are you going this morning?'

'I am going where there are rivers of wine,
The mountains bread and honey;
There Kings and Queens do mind the swine,
And the poor have all the money.'

Anon.

The Night Will Never Stay

The night will never stay,
   The night will still go by,
Though with a million stars
   You pin it to the sky,
Though you bind it with the blowing wind
   And buckle it with the moon,
The night will slip away
   Like sorrow or a tune.

Eleanor Farjeon

Some One

Some one came knocking
  At my wee, small door;
Some one came knocking,
  I'm sure – sure – sure;
I listened, I opened,
  I looked to left and right,
But nought there was a-stirring
  In the still dark night;
Only the busy beetle
  Tap-tapping in the wall,
Only from the forest
  The screech-owl's call,
Only the cricket whistling
  While the dewdrops fall,
So I know not who came knocking,
  At all, at all, at all.

Walter de la Mare

The Kitten in the Falling Snow

The year-old kitten
has never seen snow,
fallen or falling, until now
this late winter afternoon.

He sits with wide eyes
at the firelit window, sees
white things falling
from black trees.

Are they petals, leaves or birds?
They cannot be the cabbage whites
he batted briefly with his paws,
or the puffball seeds in summer grass.

They make no sound, they have no wings
and yet they can whirl and fly around
until they swoop like swallows, and
disappear into the ground.

'Where do they go?' he questions,
with eyes ablaze, following their flight
into black stone. So I put him
out into the yard, to make their acquaintance.

He has to look up at them: when one
blanches his coral nose, he sneezes,
and flicks a few from his whiskers, from
his sharpened ear, that picks up silences.

He catches one on a curled-up paw
and licks it quickly, before
its strange milk fades, then sniffs its ghost,
a wetness, while his black coat

shivers with stars of flickering frost.
He shivers at something else that makes his thin
tail swish, his fur stand on end! 'What's this? . . .'
Then he suddenly scoots in to safety

and sits again with wide eyes
at the firelit window, sees
white things falling
from black trees.

James Kirkup

The Vampire Duck

There's a vampire duck waddling about,
You can hear its ghostly quack.
Keep away from the pond at midnight
Or the feathery fiend will attack.

Brian Patten

God's Grandeur

The world is charged with the grandeur of God.
    It will flame out, like shining from shook foil;
    It gathers to a greatness, like the ooze of oil
Crushed. Why do men then now not reck his rod?
Generations have trod, have trod, have trod;
    And all is seared with trade; bleared, smeared with toil;
    And wears man's smudge and shares man's smell: the soil
Is bare now, nor can foot feel, being shod.

And for all this, nature is never spent;
   There lives the dearest freshness deep down things;
And though the last lights off the black West went
   Oh, morning, at the brown brink eastward, springs –
Because the Holy Ghost over the bent
   World broods with warm breast and with ah! bright wings.

Gerard Manley Hopkins

Kate's Unicorn

I saw a unicorn in the garden,
I did, the other night,
admittedly it was twelve o'clock
but the moon was really bright

I got up to go to the toilet
looked out of the window to see
a gleaming white shape in the shadows
I'll swear that it looked up at me

It nibbled on the azaleas,
sniffed at the lilacs and then
started in on Dad's dahlias
and looked up at the window again

I tried to call downstairs quietly
but they couldn't hear for the TV
So I tiptoed to the back door
but he'd gone: there was nothing to see

Next day I looked in the garden
there were hoofmarks on the flowerbeds,
some broken lilac-branches
and withered dahlia heads

Each night now I look through the window
when the moon is full and round
did I see something move in the shadows,
hear a distant, neighing sound?

Mum and Dad and the others all tell me
I'm the biggest liar ever born
But I know that he'll come back to see me soon,
my midnight unicorn.

Adrian Henri

Twos

Lots of things come in twos –
Ears and earmuffs, feet and shoes,
Ankles, shoulders, elbows, eyes,
Heels and shins and knees and thighs,
Gumboots, ice skates, mittens, socks,
Humps on camels, hands on clocks.
And heads on monsters also do –
Like that one . . .
Hiding right behind you!

Jeff Moss

Shallow Poem

I've thought of a poem.
I carry it carefully,
nervously, in my head,
like a saucer of milk;
in case I should spill some lines
before I can put it down.

Gerda Mayer

Animal Rights

Our cat
Won't use the cat-flap
Any more.
He's started to fight
For his Animal Rights
And insists
That he uses the door.

Lindsay MacRae

Heroes

Heroes are funny people, dey are lost an found
Sum heroes are brainy an sum are muscle-bound,
Plenty heroes die poor an are heroes after dying
Sum heroes mek yu smile when yu feel like crying.
Sum heroes are made heroes as a political trick
Sum heroes are sensible an sum are very thick!
Sum heroes are not heroes cause dey do not play de game
A hero can be young or old and have a silly name.
Drunks an sober types alike hav heroes of dere kind
Most heroes are heroes out of sight an out of mind,
Sum heroes shine a light upon a place where darkness fell
Yu could be a hero soon, yes, yu can never tell.
So if yu see a hero, better treat dem wid respect
Poets an painters say heroes are a prime subject,
Most people hav heroes even though some don't admit
I say we're all heroes if we do our little bit.

Benjamin Zephaniah

The Song of Wandering Aengus

I went out to the hazel wood,
Because a fire was in my head,
And cut and peeled a hazel wand,
And hooked a berry to a thread;
And when white moths were on the wing,
And moth-like stars were flickering out,
I dropped the berry in a stream
And caught a little silver trout.

When I had laid it on the floor
I went to blow the fire a-flame,
But something rustled on the floor,
And someone called me by my name:
It had become a glimmering girl
With apple blossom in her hair
Who called me by my name and ran
And faded through the brightening air.

Though I am old with wandering
Through hollow lands and hilly lands,
I will find out where she has gone,
And kiss her lips and take her hands;
And walk among long dappled grass,
And pluck till time and times are done
The silver apples of the moon,
The golden apples of the sun.

W.B. Yeats

Calico Pie

Calico Pie,
  The little Birds fly
Down to the calico tree,
  Their wings were blue,
  And they sang 'Tilly-loo!'
Till away they flew, –
    And they never came back to me!
      They never came back!
      They never came back!
    They never came back to me!

Calico Jam,
The little Fish swam,
Over the syllabub sea,
He took off his hat,
To the Sole and the Sprat,
And the Willeby-wat, –
But he never came back to me!
He never came back!
He never came back!
He never came back to me!

Calico Ban,
The little Mice ran,
To be ready in time for tea,
Flippity flup,
They drank it all up,
And danced in the cup, –
But they never came back to me!
They never came back!
They never came back!
They never came back to me!

Calico Drum,
The Grasshoppers come,
The Butterfly, Beetle, and Bee,
Over the ground
Around and round,
With a hop and a bound, –
But they never came back!
They never came back!
They never came back!
They never came back to me!

Edward Lear

Snowdrops

I like to think
That, long ago,
There fell to earth
Some flakes of snow
Which loved this cold,
Grey world of ours
So much, they stayed
As snowdrop flowers.

Mary Vivian

The Cat's Muse

> *And the fat*
> *cat musing on the mat*
> *sang*
>
> *(flat):*

I'm a tabby flabby house cat, just a fusty ball of fur,
A never-caught-a-mouse cat with a rusty sort of purr.
But sit down on the hearth mat and watch the fire with me.
I'll show you some of the dark and wild cats up my family
 tree.

> Oh I'm no common-or-garden cat.
> There's something you might miss:
> the sabre teeth that I unsheath
> when I stretch and yawn like this.

Sheba was a temple cat in Tutankhamun's days.
She had a hundred priestesses and several hundred slaves.
She curled up on an altar on a bed of purple silk,
Off saucers made of beaten gold she dined on camel's milk.

Oh I'm no common-or-garden cat.
My pedigree tends to show.
My tail is like a cobra
when it lashes to and fro.

Captain Moggan was a ship's cat and he sailed the Spanish Main.
He went all the way around Cape Horn and made it home again.
His claws were sharp as cutlasses. His life was sharp and short.
He died in Valparaiso, leaving kittens in every port.

Oh I'm no common-or-garden cat.
Haven't you noticed my
one lop ear like a pirate's hat
that flops across my eye?

Greymalkin was a black magic cat with fur as slick as pitch.
She held covens in a cavern with a wild and wicked witch.
And when she went out hunting on a moonlit winter's night
The village folk would bar their doors and dogs dropped dead with fright.

Oh I'm no common-or-garden cat.
Who knows what I might do?
You'd better keep me happy
or I'll put a spell . . .

         . . . on . . .

            . . . YOU!

Philip Gross

Sir's a Secret Agent

Sir's a secret agent
He's licensed to thrill
At Double-Oh Sevening
He's got bags of skill.

He's tall, dark and handsome
With a muscular frame
Teaching's his profession
But Danger's his game!

He's cool and he's calm
When he makes a decision
He's a pilot, sky-diver
And can teach long-division.

No mission's too big
No mission's too small
Schoolkids, mad scientists
He takes care of them all.

He sorts out the villains
The spies and the crooks
Then comes back to school
And marks all our books!

Tony Langham

To a Haggis

Fair fa' your honest sonsie face,
Great chieftain o' the puddin'-race!
Aboon them a' ye tak your place,
  Painch, tripe, or thairm:
Weel are ye wordy o' a grace
  As lang's my arm.

The groaning trencher there ye fill,
Your hurdies like a distant hill;
Your pin wad help to mend a mill
  In time o' need;
While thro' your pores the dews distil
  Like amber bead.

His knife see rustic Labour dight,
An' cut you up wi' ready sleight,
Trenching your gushing entrails bright
  Like ony ditch;
And then, O what a glorious sight,
  Warm-reekin', rich!

Then, horn for horn they stretch an' strive,
Deil tak the hindmost! on they drive,
Till a' their weel-swall'd kytes belyve
     Are bent like drums;
Then auld guidman, maist like to rive,
     Bethankit hums.

Is there that o'er his French ragout,
Or olio that wad staw a sow,
Or fricassee wad mak her spew
     Wi' perfect sconner,
Looks down wi' sneering scornfu' view
     On sic a dinner?

Poor devil! See him owre his trash,
As feckless as a wither'd rash,
His spindle shank a guid whip-lash,
     His nieve a nit:
Thro' bloody flood or field to dash,
     O how unfit!

But mark the Rustic, haggis-fed –
The trembling earth resounds his tread!
Clap in his walie nieve a blade,
     He'll mak it whissle;
An' legs, an' arms, an' heads will sned,
     Like taps o' thrissle.

Ye Pow'rs, wha mak mankind your care,
And dish them out their bill o' fare,
Auld Scotland wants nae skinking ware
      That jaups in luggies;
But, if ye wish her gratefu' prayer,
      Gie her a Haggis!

Robert Burns

Thaw

Over the land freckled with snow half-thawed
The speculating rooks at their nests cawed
And saw from elm-tops, delicate as flower of grass,
What we below could not see, Winter pass.

Edward Thomas

Grumbly Moon

'Turn that music down!'
Shouted the grumbly moon to
The rock 'n' roll stars.

Brian Patten

Stop all the Clocks

Stop all the clocks, cut off the telephone,
Prevent the dog from barking with a juicy bone,
Silence the pianos and with muffled drum
Bring out the coffin, let the mourners come.

Let aeroplanes circle moaning overhead
Scribbling on the sky the message He is Dead.
Put crêpe bows round the white necks of the public doves,
Let the traffic policemen wear black cotton gloves.

He was my North, my South, my East and West,
My working week and my Sunday rest,
My noon, my midnight, my talk, my song;
I thought that love would last for ever: I was wrong.

The stars are not wanted now: put out every one,
Pack up the moon and dismantle the sun,
Pour away the ocean and sweep up the wood;
For nothing now can ever come to any good.

W.H. Auden

Seasons

In Springtime when the leaves are young,
Clear dewdrops gleam like jewels, hung
On boughs the fair birds roost among.

When Summer comes with sweet unrest,
Birds weary of their mother's breast,
And look abroad and leave the nest.

In Autumn ere the waters freeze,
The swallows fly across the seas: –
If we could fly away with these!

In Winter when the birds are gone,
The sun himself looks starved and wan,
And starved the snow he shines upon.

Christina Rossetti

The Lost Angels

In a fish tank in France
we discovered the lost angels,
fallen from heaven and floating now
on imaginary tides.
And all along the sides of the tank,
faces peered, leered at them,
laughing, pouting,
pointing, shouting,
while hung above their heads, a sign,
'Ne pas plonger les mains dans le bassin.'
Don't put your hands in the tank
– the turtles bite seriously.
And who can blame them,
these creatures with angels' wings,
drifting past like alien craft.
Who knows what signals they send
through an imitation ocean,
out of sight of sky,
out of touch with stars?

Dream on, lost angels,
then one day, one glorious day,
you'll flap your wings
and fly again.

Brian Moses

For Johnny

Do not despair
For Johnny-head-in-air;
He sleeps as sound
As Johnny under ground.

Fetch out no shroud
For Johnny-in-the-cloud;
And keep your tears
For him in after years.

Better by far
For Johnny-the-bright-star,
To keep your head,
And see his children fed.

John Pudney

February

Problems in the School of Fish
(An Inquisition with Fish In)

On the whole, would you say that a solo sole
should enrol in a shoal of sole?
Do the venomous antennae of anemones
menace many of their eminent enemies?

Well, I turned aside and sighed and denied it,
as a slighty short-sighted light-shy sea-slug
shrugged, wide-eyed, undecided.

Shall our six sick sharks, shivery and sallow,
seek shelter in the shadows of sandy shallows?
Is its purpleness surplus to the purpose of a porpoise?
Is the shorter sort of shore-turtle sure to be a tortoise?

Well, I turned aside and sighed and denied it,
while the slightly short-sighted light-shy sea-slug
shrugged, wide-eyed, undecided.

Should sea-shore shrimps shun sunshine?
And if it's customary to trust crustaceans,
surely surly shellfish shouldn't be so selfish?

As I turned aside and I sighed and denied it,
the slightly short-sighted light-shy sea-slug
still shrugged, wide-eyed, undecided.

Nick Toczek

Us Two

Wherever I am, there's always Pooh,
There's always Pooh and Me.
Whatever I do, he wants to do,
'Where are you going today?' says Pooh:
'Well, that's very odd 'cos I was too.
Let's go together,' says Pooh, says he.
'Let's go together,' says Pooh.

'What's twice eleven?' I said to Pooh,
('Twice what?' said Pooh to Me.)
'I *think* it ought to be twenty-two.'
'Just what I think myself,' said Pooh.
'It wasn't an easy sum to do,
But that's what it is,' said Pooh, said he.
'That's what it is,' said Pooh.

'Let's look for dragons,' I said to Pooh.
'Yes, let's,' said Pooh to Me.
We crossed the river and found a few –
'Yes, those are dragons all right,' said Pooh.
'As soon as I saw their beaks I knew.
That's what they are,' said Pooh, said he.
'That's what they are,' said Pooh.

'Let's frighten the dragons,' I said to Pooh.
'That's right,' said Pooh to Me.
'*I'm* not afraid,' I said to Pooh,
And I held his paw and I shouted, 'Shoo!
Silly old dragons!' – and off they flew.
'I wasn't afraid,' said Pooh, said he,
'I'm *never* afraid with you.'

So wherever I am, there's always Pooh,
There's always Pooh and Me.
'What would I do?' I said to Pooh,
'If it wasn't for you,' and Pooh said: 'True,
It isn't much fun for One, but Two
Can stick together,' says Pooh, says he.
'That's how it is,' says Pooh.

A.A. Milne

There was an Old Man of Dumbree

There was an Old Man of Dumbree,
Who taught little Owls to drink Tea;
   For he said, 'To eat mice
   Is not proper or nice,'
That amiable Man of Dumbree.

Edward Lear

Out in the Desert

Out in the desert lies the sphinx
It never eats and it never drinx
Its body quite solid without any chinx
And when the sky's all purples and pinx
(As if it was painted with coloured inx)
And the sun it ever so swiftly sinx
Behind the hills in a couple of twinx
You may hear (if you're lucky) a bell that clinx
And also tolls and also tinx
And they say at the very same sound the sphinx
It sometimes smiles and it sometimes winx:

But nobody knows just what it thinx.

Charles Causley

My Baby Brother's Secrets

When my baby brother
wants to tell me a secret,
he comes right up close.
But instead of putting his lips
against my ear,
he presses his ear
tightly against my ear.
Then, he whispers so softly
that I can't hear
a word he is saying.

My baby brother's secrets
are safe with me.

John Foster

Cinquain Prayer, February Night

On this
cold night I kneel
with thanks for catkins, pale
green under the lamplight by the
roadside.

Fred Sedgwick

Sweet Music's Power

Orpheus with his lute made trees
And the mountain tops that freeze
   Bow themselves when he did sing:
To his music plants and flowers
Ever sprung; as sun and showers
   There had made a lasting spring.

Every thing that heard him play,
Even the billows of the sea,
   Hung their heads and then lay by.
In sweet music is such art,
Killing care and grief of heart
   Fall asleep, or hearing, die.

William Shakespeare

Last Waltz

Solo was a Dodo
the last one in the land.
She didn't go to parties
or dance to birdland bands.
She hadn't got a partner,
she hadn't got a friend,
until –
   she met a Panda,
   a Pandaman called Ben.

Will you dance with me? asked Solo
Can we be a party pair?
Will you take a sprig of blossom
   – will you weave it in my hair?
Will you hold me very tightly?
   – can I hold you to my breast?
   – can I snuggle really closely
     upon your hairy chest?

The woodland flutes played softly,
the evening sang its charms
   to a Panda dancing slowly
     with a Dodo
     in its arms.

Peter Dixon

Wynken, Blynken, and Nod

Wynken, Blynken, and Nod one night
  Sailed off in a wooden shoe –
Sailed on a river of crystal light,
  Into a sea of dew.
'Where are you going, and what do you wish?'
  The old moon asked the three.
'We have come to fish for the herring fish
  That live in this beautiful sea;
  Nets of silver and gold have we!'
Said Wynken,
Blynken,
And Nod.

The old moon laughed and sang a song,
    As they rocked in the wooden shoe,
And the wind that sped them all night long
    Ruffled the waves of dew.
The little stars were the herring fish
    That lived in that beautiful sea –
'Now cast your nets wherever you wish –
    Never afeard are we';
    So cried the stars to the fishermen three:
Wynken,
Blynken,
And Nod.

All night long their nets they threw
    To the stars in the twinkling foam –
Then down from the skies came the wooden shoe,
    Bringing the fishermen home;
'Twas all so pretty a sail it seemed
    As if it could not be,
And some folks thought 'twas a dream they'd dreamed
    Of sailing that beautiful sea –
    But I shall name you the fishermen three:
Wynken,
Blynken,
And Nod.

Wynken and Blynken are two little eyes,
   And Nod is a little head,
And the wooden shoe that sailed the skies
   Is a wee one's trundle-bed.
So shut your eyes while your mother sings
   Of wonderful sights that be,
And you shall see the beautiful things
   As you rock in the misty sea,
   Where the old shoe rocked the fishermen three:
Wynken,
Blynken,
And Nod.

Eugene Field

Fame

Sound, sound the clarion, fill the fife!
   To all the sensual world proclaim,
One crowded hour of glorious life
   Is worth an age without a name.

Sir Walter Scott

Assembly

I don't want to see any racing in the corridor,
a gentle glide's what we expect in here;
not that I mind a little heavy-handed fear
but you high spirits must slow down.

And I've had complaints that some of you
slip out at playtime. Let it be quite clear
that you stay in the graveyard till you hear
the bell. The chippy's out of bounds,
so is the sweetshop and your other favourite haunts.
I'll stop your little fun and groans:
there'll be a year's detention in the dungeons
for anyone caught chewing anything but bones.

And we'll have no more silly tricks with slamming doors,
at your age you should be walking through the walls.
And it isn't nice to use your loose heads as footballs
or vanish when you're being spoken to.

And finally, I really must remind you
that moans are not allowed before midnight,
especially near the staffroom. It's impolite
and disturbs the creatures – I mean teachers –
resting in despair and mournful gloom.
You there – stop wriggling in your coffin, I can't
bear to see a scruffy ghost –
put your face back where it was this instant
or you won't get to go howling at the moon.

Class Three, instead of double Shrieking
you'll do Terminal Disease with Dr Cyst;
Class Two stays here for Creepy Sneaking.
The rest of you can go. School dismissed.

Dave Calder

The Cock Crows in the Morn

The cock crows in the morn
To tell us to rise,
And he that lies late
Will never be wise:
For early to bed,
And early to rise,
Is the way to be healthy
And wealthy and wise.

Anon.

The Dark Avenger
for 2 voices

My dog is called The Dark Avenger.
Hello, I'm Cuddles.

She understands every word I say.
Woof?

Last night I took her for a walk.
Woof! Walkies! Let's go!

Cleverly, she kept three paces ahead.
I dragged him along behind me.

She paused at every danger, spying out the land.
I stopped at every lamp-post.

When the coast was clear, she sped on.
I slipped my lead and ran away.

Scenting danger, Avenger investigated.
I found some fresh chip papers in the bushes.

I followed, every sense alert.
*He blundered through the trees, shouting 'Oi, come 'ere!
  Where are you?'*

February

Something – maybe a sixth sense – told me to stop.
He tripped over me in the dark.

There was a pale menacing figure ahead of us.
Then I saw the white Scottie from next door.

Avenger sprang into battle, eager to defend her master.
Never could stand terriers!

They fought like tigers.
We scrapped like dogs.

Until the enemy was defeated.
Till Scottie's owner pulled him off – spoilsport!

Avenger gave a victory salute.
I rolled in the puddles.

And came to check I was all right.
I shook mud over him.

'Stop it, you stupid dog!'
He congratulated me.

Sometimes, even The Dark Avenger can go too far.
Woof!!

Trevor Millum

The Bargain

My true love hath my heart, and I have his,
  By just exchange, one for the other given.
I hold his dear, and mine he cannot miss,
  There never was a better bargain driven.
His heart in me keeps me and him in one,
  My heart in him his thoughts and senses guides;
He loves my heart, for once it was his own,
  I cherish his, because in me it bides.
His heart his wound receivèd from my sight,
  My heart was wounded with his wounded heart;
For as from me on him his hurt did light,
  So still methought in me his hurt did smart.
    Both equal hurt, in this change sought our bliss:
    My true love hath my heart and I have his.

Sir Philip Sidney

The Sun has Burst the Sky

The sun has burst the sky
Because I love you
And the river its banks.

The sea laps the great rocks
Because I love you
And takes no heed of the moon dragging it away
And saying coldly 'Constancy is not for you.'

The blackbird fills the air
Because I love you
With spring and lawns and shadows falling on lawns.

The people walk in the street and laugh
I love you
And far down the river ships sound their hooters
Crazy with joy because I love you.

Jenny Joseph

A Nail

For want of a nail, the shoe was lost;
For want of a shoe, the horse was lost;
For want of a horse, the rider was lost;
For want of a rider, the battle was lost;
For want of a battle, the kingdom was lost:
And all for want of a horseshoe nail.

Anon.

Typewriting Class

Dear Miss Hinson
I am spitting
in front of my top ratter
With the rest of my commercesnail sturdy students
Triping you this later.
The truce is Miss Hinson
I am not hippy wiht my cross.
Every day on Woundsday
I sit in my dusk
With my type rutter
Trooping without lurking at the lattice
All sorts of weird messengers.
To give one exam pill,
'The quick down socks . . .
The quick brine pox . . .
The sick frown box . . .
The sick down jocks
Humps over the hazy bog'
When everyone kows
That a sick down jock
would not be seen dead
Near a hazy bog.
Another one we tripe is:

'Now is the tame
For all guide men
To cram to the head
Of the pratty.'
To may why of sinking
I that is all you get to tripe
In true whelks of sturdy
Then I am thinking of changing
To crookery classes.
I would sooner end up a crook
Than a shirt hand trappist
Any die of the wink.
I have taken the tremble, Miss Hinson
To trip you this later
So that you will be able
To understand my indignation.
I must clothe now
As the Bill is groaning

Yours fitfully . . .

Gareth Owen

Nursery Rhyme

Sing a song of nothing
with a pocket full of hand,
watch the monkey dancing
with a penguin on the sand.

See the flying rhino
eat a wrinkled peach;
the Queen of Hearts is riding by,
she's travelling to the beach.

Five and twenty donkeys
sit in a cabbage patch,
singing sailors' ditties
and watching mothballs hatch

The poet ends his reading,
he thinks he is alone,
so all the trees pull up their skirts
and make a dash for home.

Robin Mellor

The Hurt Boy and the Birds

The hurt boy talked to the birds
and fed them the crumbs of his heart.

It was not easy to find the words
for secrets he hid under his skin.
The hurt boy spoke of a bully's fist
that made his face a bruised moon –
his spectacles stamped to ruin.

It was not easy to find the words
for things that nightly hissed
as if his pillow was a hideaway for creepy-crawlies –
the note sent to the girl he fancied
held high in mockery.

But the hurt boy talked to the birds
and their feathers gave him welcome –

Their wings taught him new ways to become.

John Agard

Teeth

English Teeth, English Teeth!
Shining in the sun
A part of British heritage
Aye, each and every one.

English Teeth, Happy Teeth!
Always having fun
Clamping down on bits of fish
And sausages half done.

English Teeth! HEROES' Teeth!
Hear them click! and clack!
Let's sing a song of praise to them –
Three Cheers for the Brown Grey and Black.

Spike Milligan

Weasels

He should have been at school
but instead, he was in bed,
his room more cheerful, brighter,
sheets and pillows whiter
than they'd ever been before.

Comics, bread with crusts cut off,
a jug of homemade lemonade,
Mum's hand so cool against his brow.
Now he had her to himself at last
he'd never want to go to school again.

And all because of little spots,
he raised his vest and thanked them.
Crimson pinpricks on his chest
– some clustered, some quite lonely –
like baby strawberries or beetroot.

Dr Croker joked and felt his muscles.
'Superman! You'll soon be right as rain.'
But his voice from down the stairs
was stern and rather solemn
– and Mummy's sounded scared.

He strained to hear the words,
but they were speaking low. He slipped
out of bed, tiptoed to the door,
pressed his ear against the floor.
'Weasels. He's got weasels, I'm afraid.'

Weasels! He lay in bed and trembled.
Weasels. Furry-grey with pointed teeth.
They must have crept in as he slept,
gnawed and nibbled through the night.
He wondered how much of him was left.

His foot itched. Was it a hidden weasel?
Ankle, knee. Lots of them were there!
He screamed and she came flying.
Her arms were safe as blankets.
He didn't want to stop crying for a while.

John Latham

Rain

The rain is raining all around,
   It falls on field and tree,
It rains on the umbrellas here,
   And on the ships at sea.

Robert Louis Stevenson

O What is that Sound?

O what is that sound which so thrills the ear
   Down in the valley drumming, drumming?
Only the scarlet soldiers, dear,
   The soldiers coming.

O what is that light I see flashing so clear
  Over the distance brightly, brightly?
Only the sun on their weapons, dear,
  As they step lightly.

O what are they doing with all that gear;
  What are they doing this morning, this morning?
Only the usual manoeuvres, dear,
  Or perhaps a warning.

O why have they left the road down there;
  Why are they suddenly wheeling, wheeling?
Perhaps a change in the orders, dear;
  Why are you kneeling?

O haven't they stopped for the doctor's care;
  Haven't they reined their horses, their horses?
Why, they are none of them wounded, dear,
  None of these forces.

O is it the parson they want with white hair;
  Is it the parson, is it, is it?
No, they are passing his gateway, dear,
  Without a visit.

O it must be the farmer who lives so near;
  It must be the farmer so cunning, so cunning;
They have passed the farm already, dear,
  And now they are running.

O where are you going? stay with me here!
  Were the vows you swore me deceiving, deceiving?
No, I promised to love you, dear,
  But I must be leaving.

O it's broken the lock and splintered the door,
  O it's the gate where they're turning, turning;
Their feet are heavy on the floor
  And their eyes are burning.

W.H. Auden

The Friendly Cinnamon Bun

Shining in his stickiness and glistening with honey,
Safe among his sisters and his brothers on a tray,
With raisin eyes that looked at me as I put down my money,
There smiled a friendly cinnamon bun, and this I heard him
  say:

'It's a lovely, lovely morning, and the world's a lovely place;
I know it's going to be a lovely day.
I know we're going to be good friends; I like your honest
    face;
Together we might go a long, long way.'

The baker's girl rang up the sale, 'I'll wrap your bun,' said
    she.
'Oh no, you needn't bother,' I replied.
I smiled back at that cinnamon bun and ate him, one two
    three,
And walked out with his friendliness inside.

Russell Hoban

Secret Affair

Our love is like
a red, red
nose,
embarrassing
and somehow
conspicuous

let's hope
we don't
blow it

Andrew Rumsey

No Bread

I wish I'd made a list
I forgot to get the bread.
If I forget it again
I'll be dead.

We had blank and butter pudding,
beans on zip.
Boiled egg with deserters,
no chip butty: just chip.

I wish I'd made a list
I forgot to get the bread.
My mam got the empty bread bin
and wrapped it round my head.

Our jam sarnies were just jam
floating on the air.
We spread butter on the table
cos the bread wasn't there.

My mam says if I run away
she knows I won't be missed,
not like the bread was . . .
I wish I'd made a list!

Ian McMillan

Just in Case

When it's nearly my birthday
And so that people won't be upset
Or forget,
I always think it's kinder,
Just as a reminder,
To leave notes on plates,
Hinting at dates.

Max Fatchen

Ducks' Ditty

All along the backwater,
Through the rushes tall,
Ducks are a-dabbling,
Up tails all!

Ducks' tails, drakes' tails,
Yellow feet a-quiver,
Yellow bills all out of sight
Busy in the river!

Slushy green undergrowth
Where the roach swim –
Here we keep our larder,
Cool and full and dim!

Every one for what he likes!
We like to be
Heads down, tails up,
Dabbling free!

High in the blue above
Swifts whirl and call –
We are down a-dabbling
Up tails all!

Kenneth Grahame

March

MARCH ingorders

Winter has been sacked
for negligence

It appears he left
the sun on all day

Roger McGough

Pop Goes the Weasel!

Half a pound of tuppenny rice,
　Half a pound of treacle,
Mix it up and make it nice,
　Pop goes the weasel!

Anon.

The Sands of Dee

'O Mary, go and call the cattle home,
　And call the cattle home,
　And call the cattle home
Across the sands of Dee.'
The western wind was wild and dank with foam,
　And all alone went she.

The western tide crept up along the sand,
    And o'er and o'er the sand
    And round and round the sand,
  As far as eye could see.
The rolling mist came down and hid the land;
  And never home came she.

'Oh! is it weed, or fish, or floating hair –
    A tress of golden hair,
    A drowned maiden's hair
  Above the nets at sea?
Was never salmon yet that shone so fair
  Among the stakes on Dee.'

They rowed her in across the rolling foam,
    The cruel crawling foam,
    The cruel hungry foam,
  To her grave beside the sea:
But still the boatmen hear her call the cattle home
  Across the sands of Dee.

Charles Kingsley

Isn't it Amazing?

Now isn't it amazing
That seeds grow into flowers,
That grubs become bright butterflies
And rainbows come from showers,
That busy bees make honey gold
And never spend time lazing,
That eggs turn into singing birds,
Now isn't that amazing?

Max Fatchen

I Saw a Ship A-Sailing

I saw a ship a-sailing,
  A-sailing on the sea,
And oh but it was laden
  With pretty things for me.

There were comfits in the cabin,
  And apples in the hold;
The sails were made of silk,
  And the masts were all of gold.

The four-and-twenty sailors,
  That stood between the decks,
Were four-and-twenty white mice
  With chains about their necks.

The captain was a duck
  With a packet on his back,
And when the ship began to move
  The captain said Quack! Quack!

Anon.

Secret Love

Chalked on a wall in the playground,
These words inside a heart:
'David loves Susan for ever,
And we shall never part.'

But nobody knew, and nobody guessed,
The secret behind what it said:
That Dave was the History teacher,
And Sue was the Deputy Head.

Mike Jubb

A Date with Spring

Got a date with Spring
Got to look me best.
Of all the trees
I'll be the smartest dressed.

Perfumed breeze
behind me ear.
Pollen accessories
all in place.
Raindrop moisturizer
for me face.
Sunlight tints
to spruce up the hair.

What's the good of being a tree
if you can't flaunt your beauty?

Winter, I was naked.
Exposed as can be.
Me wardrobe took off
with the wind.
Life was a frosty slumber.
Now, Spring, here I come.

Can't wait to slip in
to me little green number.

John Agard

The Rainbow

Boats sail on the rivers,
    And ships sail on the seas;
But clouds that sail across the sky
    Are prettier far than these.

There are bridges on the rivers,
    As pretty as you please;
But the bow that bridges heaven,
    And overtops the trees,
And builds a road from earth to sky,
    Is prettier far than these.

Christina Rossetti

Glenis

The teacher says:

Why is it, Glenis,
Please answer me this,
The only time
You ever stop talking in class
Is if I ask you
Where's the Khyber Pass?
Or when was the Battle of Waterloo?
Or what is nine times three?
Or how do you spell
Mississippi?
Why is it, Glenis,
The only time you are silent
Is when I ask you a question?

And Glenis says:

Allan Ahlberg

Rabbit's Spring

Snow
goes,

Ice
thaws,

Warm
paws!

Brian Patten

The Hippopotamus's Birthday

He has opened all his parcels
    but the largest and the last;
His hopes are at their highest
    and his heart is beating fast.
O happy Hippopotamus,
    what lovely gift is here?
He cuts the string. The world stands still.
    A pair of boots appear!

O little Hippopotamus,
    the sorrows of the small!
He dropped two tears to mingle
    with the flowing Senegal;
And the 'Thank you' that he uttered
    was the saddest ever heard
In the Senegambian jungle
    from the mouth of beast or bird.

E. V. Rieu

Cat Asks Mouse Out

Mrs Mouse
Come out of your house
It is a fine sunny day
And I am waiting to play.

Bring the little ones too
And we can run to and fro.

Stevie Smith

My Heart Leaps Up

My heart leaps up when I behold
    A rainbow in the sky:
So was it when my life began;
So is it now I am a man;
So be it when I shall grow old,
    Or let me die!
The Child is father of the Man;
And I could wish my days to be
Bound each to each by natural piety.

William Wordsworth

Ride a Cock-Horse

Ride a cock-horse
   to Banbury Cross,
To see a fine lady
   upon a white horse;
With rings on her fingers
   and bells on her toes,
She shall have music
   wherever she goes.

Anon.

March Dusk

About the hour light wobbles
Between the day and night,

On paving-stones and cobbles
Rain hisses with weak spite

And plane trees dangling bobbles,
Drip leafless from numb height

Where wounded springtime hobbles
That soon will leap with light.

Kit Wright

Poem

As the cat
climbed over
the top of

the jamcloset
first the right
forefoot

carefully
then the hind
stepped down

into the pit of
the empty
flowerpot

William Carlos Williams

Lochinvar

Oh, young Lochinvar is come out of the West, –
Through all the wide Border his steed was the best.
And, save his good broadsword, he weapon had none –
He rode all unarmed, and he rode all alone.
So faithful in love, and so dauntless in war,
There never was knight like the young Lochinvar.

He stayed not for brake, and he stopped not for stone.
He swam the Eske river where ford there was none.
But ere he alighted at Netherby gate,
The bride had consented, the gallant came late;
For a laggard in love, and a dastard in war,
Was to wed the fair Ellen of brave Lochinvar.

So boldly he entered the Netherby hall,
Among bridesmen, and kinsmen, and brothers, and all.
Then spoke the bride's father, his hand on his sword,
(For the poor craven bridegroom said never a word),
'Oh, come ye in peace here, or come ye in war,
Or to dance at our bridal, young Lord Lochinvar?'

'I long wooed your daughter, my suit you denied; –
Love swells like the Solway, but ebbs like its tide; –
And now am I come, with this lost love of mine,
To lead but one measure, drink one cup of wine.
There are maidens in Scotland more lovely by far,
That would gladly be bride to the young Lochinvar.'

The bride kissed the goblet, the knight took it up,
He quaffed off the wine, and he threw down the cup.
She looked down to blush, and she looked up to sigh,
With a smile on her lips, and a tear in her eye.
He took her soft hand ere her mother could bar:
'Now tread we a measure,' said young Lochinvar.

So stately his form, and so lovely her face,
That never a hall such a galliard did grace;
While her mother did fret, and her father did fume,
And the bridegroom stood dangling his bonnet and plume;
And the bridesmaidens whispered, ''Twere better by far
To have matched our fair cousin with young Lochinvar.'

One touch to her hand, and one word in her ear,
When they reached the hall-door, and the charger stood
    near;
So light to the croupe the fair lady he swung,
So light to the saddle before her he sprung!
'She is won! we are gone, over bank, bush, and scaur;
They'll have fleet steeds that follow,' quoth young
    Lochinvar.

There was mounting 'mong Graemes of the Netherby clan;
Forsters, Fenwicks, and Musgraves, they rode and they ran;
There was racing and chasing on Cannobie Lee,
But the lost bride of Netherby ne'er did they see.
So daring in love, and so dauntless in war,
Have ye e'er heard of gallant like young Lochinvar?

Sir Walter Scott

Ten Syllables for Spring

> daffylonglegs
> blowing
> buttered trumpets.

Sue Cowling

The Arrow and the Song

I shot an arrow into the air,
It fell to earth, I knew not where;
For, so swiftly it flew, the sight
Could not follow it in its flight.

I breathed a song into the air,
It fell to earth, I knew not where;
For who has sight so keen and strong,
That it can follow the flight of song?

Long, long afterward, in an oak
I found the arrow, still unbroke;
And the song, from beginning to end,
I found again in the heart of friend.

Henry Wadsworth Longfellow

Mary, Mary, Quite Contrary

Mary, Mary, quite contrary,
  How does your garden grow?
With silver bells and cockle shells,
  And pretty maids all in a row.

Anon.

Bruce's Address before Bannockburn

Scots, wha hae wi' Wallace bled,
Scots, wham Bruce has aften led,
Welcome to your gory bed,
   Or to victorie.

Now's the day, and now's the hour,
See the front o' battle lour!
See approach proud Edward's power –
   Chains and slaverie!

Wha will be a traitor knave?
Wha will fill a coward's grave?
Wha sae base as be a slave?
   Let him turn and flee!

March

Wha for Scotland's King and law
Freedom's sword will strongly draw,
Freeman stand, or freeman fa'.
    Let him on wi' me!

By oppression's woes and pains!
By your sons in servile chains!
We will drain our dearest veins,
    But they shall be free!

Lay the proud usurpers low!
Tyrants fall in every foe!
Liberty's in every blow!
    Let us do or die!

Robert Burns

Tell Me, Where is Fancy Bred?

Tell me, where is fancy bred,
Or in the heart, or in the head?
How begot, how nourished?
  Reply, reply.

It is engender'd in the eyes,
With gazing fed; and fancy dies
In the cradle where it lies.
  Let us all ring fancy's knell.
  I'll begin it – Ding, dong, bell.

William Shakespeare

Roman Wall Blues

Over the heather the wet wind blows,
I've lice in my tunic and a cold in my nose.

The rain comes pattering out of the sky,
I'm a Wall soldier, I don't know why.

The mist creeps over the hard grey stone,
My girl's in Tungria; I sleep alone.

Aulus goes hanging around her place,
I don't like his manners, I don't like his face.

Piso's a Christian, he worships a fish;
There'd be no kissing if he had his wish.

She gave me a ring but I diced it away;
I want my girl and I want my pay.

When I'm a veteran with only one eye
I shall do nothing but look at the sky.

W.H. Auden

The Frog who Dreamed she was an Opera Singer

There once was a frog
who dreamed she was an opera singer.
She wished so hard she grew a long throat
and a beautiful polkadot green coat
and intense opera singer's eyes.
She even put on a little weight.
But she couldn't grow tall.
She just couldn't grow tall.
She leaped to the Queen Elizabeth Hall,
practising her sonata all the way.
Her voice was promising and lovely.
She couldn't wait to leapfrog onto the stage.
What a presence on the stage!
All the audience in the Queen Elizabeth Hall
gasped to see one so small sing like that.
Her voice trembled and swelled
and filled with colour.
That frog was a green prima donna.

Jackie Kay

Timothy Winters

Timothy Winters comes to school
With eyes as wide as a football pool,
Ears like bombs and teeth like splinters:
A blitz of a boy is Timothy Winters.

His belly is white, his neck is dark,
And his hair is an exclamation mark.
His clothes are enough to scare a crow
And through his britches the blue winds blow.

When teacher talks he won't hear a word
And he shoots down dead the arithmetic-bird,
He licks the patterns off his plate
And he's not even heard of the Welfare State.

Timothy Winters has bloody feet
And he lives in a house on Suez Street,
He sleeps in a sack on the kitchen floor
And they say there aren't boys like him any more.

Old Man Winters likes his beer
And his missus ran off with a bombardier,
Grandma sits in the grate with a gin
And Timothy's dosed with an aspirin.

The Welfare Worker lies awake
But the law's as tricky as a ten-foot snake,
So Timothy Winters drinks his cup
And slowly goes on growing up.

At Morning Prayers the Master helves
For children less fortunate than ourselves,
And the loudest response in the room is when
Timothy Winters roars 'Amen!'

So come one angel, come on ten:
Timothy Winters says 'Amen
Amen amen amen amen.'
Timothy Winters, Lord.
                Amen.

Charles Causley

Spring, the Sweet Spring

Spring, the sweet spring, is the year's pleasant king;
Then blooms each thing, then maids dance in a ring,
Cold doth not sting, the pretty birds do sing,
   'Cuckoo, jug-jug, pu-we, to-witta-woo!'

The palm and may make country houses gay,
Lambs frisk and play, the shepherds pipe all day,
And we hear aye birds tune this merry lay,
   'Cuckoo, jug-jug, pu-we, to-witta-woo.'

The fields breathe sweet, the daisies kiss our feet,
Young lovers meet, old wives a-sunning sit,
In every street these tunes our ears do greet,
   'Cuckoo, jug-jug, pu-wee, to-witta-woo!'
   Spring, the sweet spring!

Thomas Nashe

The Queen of Hearts

The Queen of Hearts,
She made some tarts,
All on a summer's day;
The Knave of Hearts,
He stole the tarts,
And took them clean away!

The King of Hearts
Called for the tarts,
And beat the Knave full sore;
The Knave of Hearts
Brought back the tarts,
And vowed he'd steal no more.

Anon.

The Prayer of the Little Ducks

Dear God,
give us a flood of water.
Let it rain tomorrow and always.
Give us plenty of little slugs
and other luscious things to eat.
Protect all folk who quack
and everyone who knows how to swim.
Amen.

Carmen Bernos de Gasztold,
translated from the French by Rumer Godden

Sam Said

Sam said 'Do you know what's pink?
Flossie's sunburnt nose.'
Sam said 'Do you know what's black?
Night-time, ravens, crows.'
Sam said 'Do you know what's grey?
Uncle Archie's hair.'
Sam said 'Do you know what's white?
Brand new underwear.'
Sam said 'Do you know what's yellow?
Butter, sunshine, cheese.'
Sam said 'Do you know what's green?
Grass and pods of peas.'
Sam said 'Do you know what's orange?
Swedes and flames and carrots.'
Sam said 'Do you know what's blue?
Wings and tails of parrots.'
Sam said 'Do you know what's red?
Cherries, ketchup, Mars.'

Sam said 'Do you know what's silver?
Pins and shooting stars.'
Sam said 'Do you know what's purple?
Hot Ribena, plums.'
Sam said 'Do you know what's golden?'
'Silence,' said his chums.

Richard Edwards

Dream Team

My team
Will have all the people in it
Who're normally picked last.

Such as me.

When it's my turn to be chooser
I'll overlook Nick Magic-Feet-Jones
And Supersonic Simon Hughes

And I'll point at my best friend Sean
Who'll faint with surprise
And delight.

And at Robin who's always the one
Left at the end that no one chose –
Unless he's away, in which case it's guess who?

And Tim who can't see a thing
Without his glasses
I'll pick him.

And the rest of the guys that Mr Miller
Calls dead-legs but only need their chance
To show what they're made of.

We'll play in the cup final
In front of the class, the school, the town,
The world, the galaxy.

And due to the masterly leadership shown
By their captain, not forgetting
His three out-of-this-world goals,

We'll WIN.

Frances Nagle

from *Five Answers to the Question 'Where did Winter go?'*

Winter slunk away
like a guilty mongrel,
brought to heel by Spring.

Judith Nicholls

April

Applause

I gave my cat a six-minute standing ovation
For services rendered: hunting of very small game,

Pouncing about and sitting in cardboard boxes,
Three-legged washing and never knowing his name,

The jump on the knee, the nuzzle at night, the kneading
Of dough with his paws, the punch at the candle flame,

The yowling for food, the looking at everything otherwise,
Staring through it straight with a faraway aim.

I gave my cat a six-minute standing ovation.
Your cat's like that? I think you should do the same.

Kit Wright

Spot the Hidden Part of a Loaf

Look carefully
because within this poem
is hiddenCRUST
the name of a part
of a loaf.

ThisCRUST
part of a loaf
is just in the poem
for a laugh.

SomebodyCRUST said
to me
'I bet you can't hide
part of a loaf
in a poem.'

CRUST

Have you spotted it yet?
Have you spotted it yet?

Ian McMillan

I Know Someone Who Can

I know someone who can
take a mouthful of custard and blow it
down their nose.
I know someone who can
make their ears wiggle.
I know someone who can
shake their cheeks so it sounds
like ducks quacking.
I know someone who can
throw peanuts in the air and catch them
in their mouth.
I know someone who can
balance a pile of 12 2p pieces on his elbow
and snatch his elbow from under them
and catch them.
I know someone who can
bend her thumb back to touch her wrist.
I know someone who can
crack his nose.

I know someone who can
say the alphabet backwards.
I know someone who can put their hands in
their armpits and blow raspberries.
I know someone who can
wiggle her little toe.
I know someone who can
lick the bottom of her chin.
I know someone who can
slide their top lip one way
and their bottom lip the other way,
and that someone is
ME.

Michael Rosen

Spring

Nothing is so beautiful as spring –
　　When weeds, in wheels, shoot long and lovely and lush;
　　Thrush's eggs look little low heavens, and thrush
　Through the echoing timber does so rinse and wring
　The ear, it strikes like lightnings to hear him sing;
　The glassy pear-tree leaves and blooms, they brush
　The descending blue; that blue is all in a rush
With richness; the racing lambs too have fair their fling.

What is all this juice and all this joy?
　　A strain of the earth's sweet being in the beginning
In Eden garden. – Have, get, before it cloy,
　　Before it cloud, Christ, lord, and sour with sinning,
Innocent mind and Mayday in girl and boy,
　　Most, O maid's child, thy choice and worthy the winning.

Gerard Manley Hopkins

But These Things Also

But these things also are Spring's –
On banks by the roadside the grass
Long-dead that is greyer now
Than all the Winter it was;

The shell of a little snail bleached
In the grass; chip of flint, and mite
Of chalk; and the small birds' dung
In splashes of purest white:

All the white things a man mistakes
For earliest violets
Who seeks through Winter's ruins
Something to pay Winter's debts,

While the North blows, and starling flocks
By chattering on and on
Keep their spirits up in the mist,
And Spring's here, Winter's not gone.

Edward Thomas

Hunter Trials

It's awf'lly bad luck on Diana,
   Her ponies have swallowed their bits;
She fished down their throats with a spanner
   And frightened them all into fits.

So now she's attempting to borrow.
   Do lend her some bits, Mummy, *do*;
I'll lend her my own for tomorrow,
   But today I'll be wanting them too.

Just look at Prunella on Guzzle,
   The wizardest pony on earth;
Why doesn't she slacken his muzzle
   And tighten the breech in his girth?

I say, Mummy, there's Mrs Geyser
   And doesn't she look pretty sick?
I bet it's because Mona Lisa
   Was hit on the hock with a brick.

Miss Blewitt says Monica threw it,
   But Monica says it was Joan,
And Joan's very thick with Miss Blewitt,
   So Monica's sulking alone.

And Margaret failed in her paces,
   Her withers got tied in a noose,
So her coronet's caught in the traces
   And now all her fetlocks are loose.

Oh, it's me now. I'm terribly nervous.
   I wonder if Smudges will shy.
She's practically certain to swerve as
   Her Pelham is over one eye.

*   *   *

Oh, wasn't it naughty of Smudges?
   Oh, Mummy, I'm sick with disgust.
She threw me in front of the Judges,
   And my silly old collarbone's bust.

John Betjeman

in Just-

in Just-
spring   when the world is mud-
luscious the little
lame balloonman

whistles   far   and wee

and eddieandbill come
running from marbles and
piracies and it's
spring

when the world is puddle-wonderful

the queer
old balloonman whistles
far   and   wee
and bettyandisbel come dancing

from hop-scotch and jump-rope and

it's
spring
and
    the
        goat-footed

balloonMan   whistles
far
and
wee

e.e. cummings

Spring Magic!

What a fearless magician is Spring –
you really can't teach her a thing!
In she sneaks on a breeze,
draws the leaves from the trees . . .
just when Winter thought *he* was still King!

Judith Nicholls

Lord of the Dance

I danced in the morning
When the world was begun,
And I danced in the moon
And the stars and the sun
And I came down from heaven
And I danced on the earth –
At Bethlehem I had my birth.

Dance then wherever you may be;
I am the Lord of the Dance, said he,
I'll lead you all, wherever you may be,
I will lead you all in the Dance, said he.

I danced for the scribe
And the pharisee,
But they would not dance
And they couldn't follow me;
I danced for the fishermen,
For James and John –
They came with me
And the dance went on.

I danced on the Sabbath
And I cured the lame;
The holy people
Said it was a shame;
They whipped and they stripped
And they hung me high,
And they left me there
On a Cross to die.

I danced on a Friday
When the sky turned black –
It's hard to dance
With the devil on your back;
They buried my body
And they thought I'd gone –
But I am the dance
And I still go on.

They cut me down
And I leapt up high –
I am the life
That'll never, never die;
I'll live in you
If you'll live in me –
I am the Lord
Of the Dance, said he.

Dance then wherever you may be;
I am the Lord of the Dance, said he,
I'll lead you all, wherever you may be,
I will lead you all in the Dance, said he.

Sydney Carter

The Greengrocer's Love Song

Do you carrot all for me?
My heart beets for you.
With your turnip nose
And your radish face
You are a peach.
If we canteloupe
Lettuce marry.
Weed make a swell pear.

Anon.

Upon the Snail

She goes but softly, but she goeth sure;
  She stumbles not as stronger creatures do:
Her journey's shorter, so she may endure
  Better than they which do much further go.

She makes no noise, but stilly seizeth on
  The flower or herb appointed for her food,
The which she quietly doth feed upon,
  While others range, and gare, but find no good.

And though she doth but very softly go,
  However 'tis not fast, nor slow, but sure;
And certainly they that do travel so,
  The prize they do aim at, they do procure.

John Bunyan

Rain

There are holes in the sky
Where the rain gets in,
But they're ever so small
That's why rain is thin.

Spike Milligan

The Wise Cow Enjoys a Cloud

'Where did you sleep last night, Wise Cow?
Where did you lay your head?'

'I caught my horns on a rolling cloud
and made myself a bed,

and in the morning ate it raw
on freshly buttered bread.'

Nancy Willard

The Banks o' Doon

Ye flowery banks o' bonnie Doon,
   How can ye blume sae fair!
How can ye chant, ye little birds,
   And I sae fu' o' care!

Thou'll break my heart, thou bonnie bird
   That sings upon the bough;
Thou minds me o' the happy days
   When my fause Luve was true.

Thou'll break my heart, thou bonnie bird
   That sings beside thy mate;
For sae I sat, and sae I sang,
   And wist na o' my fate.

Aft hae I roved by bonnie Doon
   To see the woodbine twine,
And ilka bird sang o' its love;
   And sae did I o' mine.

Wi' lightsome heart I pu'd a rose,
  Frae aff its thorny tree;
And my fause luver staw the rose,
  But left the thorn wi' me.

Robert Burns

Seasons

Spring is showery, flowery, bowery;
Summer: hoppy, croppy, poppy;
Autumn: slippy, drippy, nippy;
Winter: breezy, sneezy, freezy.

Anon.

All Day Saturday

Let it sleet on Sunday,
Monday let it snow,
Let the mist on Tuesday
From the salt-sea flow.
Let it hail on Wednesday,
Thursday let it rain,
Let the wind on Friday
Blow a hurricane,
But Saturday, Saturday
Break fair and fine
And all day Saturday
Let the sun shine.

Charles Causley

Psalm 121

I will lift up mine eyes unto the hills, from whence cometh
my help.

My help cometh from the Lord, which made heaven and
earth.

He will not suffer thy foot to be moved: he that keepeth thee
will not slumber.

Behold, he that keepeth Israel shall neither slumber nor
sleep.

The Lord is thy keeper: the Lord is thy shade upon thy right
hand.

The sun shall not smite thee by day, nor the moon by night.

The Lord shall preserve thee from all evil: he shall preserve
thy soul.

The Lord shall preserve thy going out and thy coming in
from this time forth, and even for evermore.

The Bible

Wings

If I had wings
  I would touch the fingertips of clouds
    and glide on the wind's breath.

If I had wings
  I would taste a chunk of the sun
    as hot as peppered curry.

If I had wings
  I would listen to the clouds of sheep bleat
    that graze on the blue.

If I had wings
   I would breathe deep and sniff
     the scent of raindrops.

If I had wings
   I would gaze at the people
     who cling to the earth's crust.

If I had wings
   I would dream of
     swimming the deserts
       and walking the seas.

Pie Corbett

The Un-developers

The little cats sit under the hedge
The many small offspring of a great big tabby
Who lives out of sight round the other side of the house.
They are watching the pigeons in the road.
The pigeons strut and flirt and think no danger.
Children are delighted with the cats
And cajole them as they are tugged along by Mum;
An old woman puts down crumbs for the birds
And cars pass in between.
The cats purr and the pigeons peck up the fodder
But they are waiting for interruptions of humans to pass
So they can get on with what they are doing:
Five little kittens lurking and stalking big birds
And foolish pigeons flirt-flirting in the road.

Jenny Joseph

from *Ye Wearie Wayfarer*

Question not, but live and labour
  Till yon goal be won,
Helping every feeble neighbour,
  Seeking help from none;
Life is mostly froth and bubble,
  Two things stand like stone,
Kindness in another's trouble,
  Courage in your own.

Adam Lindsay Gordon

Where Teachers Keep their Pets

Mrs Cox has a fox
nesting in her curly locks.

Mr Spratt's tabby cat
sleeps beneath his bobble hat.

Miss Cahoots has various newts
swimming in her zip-up boots.

Mr Spry has Fred his fly
eating food stains from his tie.

Mrs Groat shows off her stoat
round the collar of her coat.

Mr Spare's got grizzly bears
hiding in his spacious flares.

And . . .

Mrs Vickers has a stick insect called 'Stickers'
. . . but no one's ever seen where she keeps it.

Paul Cookson

The Magical Mouse

I am the magical mouse
I don't eat cheese
I eat sunsets
And the tops of trees

I don't wear fur

I wear funnels
Of lost ships and the weather
That's under dead leaves
I am the magical mouse

I don't fear cats

Or woodsowls
I do as I please
Always
I don't eat crusts
I am the magical mouse
I eat
Little birds and maidens

That taste like dust.

Kenneth Patchen

James had a Magic Set for Christmas

James had practised the tricks for days
but in front of the class
they all went wrong.
The invisible penny
dropped from his sleeve,
the secret pocket
failed to open,
his magic wand broke.
'Perhaps another time,' Miss Burroughs suggested,
'another day
when you've the hang of it.'

'No, Miss! Please!
I can do them, honestly.'

Suddenly
a white rabbit was sitting
on Miss Burroughs' table,
a green snake, tongue flicking,
scattered the class from the carpet,
the school was showered with golden coins
that rolled into piles on the playground.
'But, James!' Miss Burroughs said. 'Shouldn't—'
There was a flash of lightning.

While the fire brigade coaxed
Miss Burroughs down from the oak
she'd flown into
on the other side of the playground,
the caretaker quietly swept up the mess
and Mr Pinner, the headmaster,
confiscated the magic set.
'A rather dangerous toy,' he said, 'James!'

James is still asking for it back.

Brian Morse

Buttercups and Daisies

Buttercups and daisies,
　Oh what pretty flowers,
Coming in the springtime
　To tell of sunny hours.
While the trees are leafless,
　While the fields are bare,
Buttercups and daisies
　Spring up everywhere.

Anon.

It was a Lover and his Lass

It was a lover and his lass,
   With a hey, and a ho, and a hey nonino,
That o'er the green corn field did pass
   In springtime, the only pretty ring time,
When birds do sing, hey ding a ding, ding:
Sweet lovers love the spring.

Between the acres of the rye,
   With a hey, and a ho, and a hey nonino,
These pretty country folks would lie,
   In springtime, the only pretty ring time,
When birds do sing, hey ding a ding, ding:
Sweet lovers love the spring.

This carol they began that hour,
   With a hey, and a ho, and a hey nonino,
How that a life was but a flower
   In springtime, the only pretty ring time,
When birds do sing, hey ding a ding, ding:
Sweet lovers love the spring.

And therefore take the present time,
    With a hey, and a ho, and a hey nonino;
For love is crownèd with the prime
    In springtime, the only pretty ring time,
When birds do sing, hey ding a ding, ding:
Sweet lovers love the spring.

                      William Shakespeare

Skye Boat Song

Sing me a song of a lad that is gone,
    Say, could that lad be I?
Merry of soul he sailed on a day
    Over the sea to Skye.

Mull was astern, Rum on the port,
    Eigg on the starboard bow;
Glory of youth glowed in his soul:
    Where is that glory now?

Sing me a song of a lad that is gone,
    Say, could that lad be I?
Merry of soul he sailed on a day
    Over the sea to Skye.

Give me again all that was there,
    Give me the sun that shone!
Give me the eyes, give me the soul,
    Give me the lad that's gone!

Sing me a song of a lad that is gone,
    Say, could that lad be I?
Merry of soul he sailed on a day
    Over the sea to Skye.

Billow and breeze, islands and seas,
    Mountains of rain and sun,
All that was good, all that was fair,
    All that was me is gone.

Robert Louis Stevenson

Talking-tubes

I believe everything my brother tells me
that's why I know about talking-tubes in old houses.

Once we went to this old house
and the guide who was taking us round
told us that there were tubes
running through the massive great thick walls
so that the people in the olden days
could talk to each other.

After the guide went off
my brother explained to me
that these talking-tubes were only discovered
a short while ago.
He said they were closed up
with great big corks.

He said,
when the people who discovered them
pulled the corks out
they heard
all these old words from hundreds of years ago.
They heard knights-in-armour talking.
What they said just came tumbling out of the talking-tubes.
Amazing.

I believe everything my brother tells me
that's why I know about talking-tubes in old houses.

Michael Rosen

O Captain! My Captain!

O Captain! my Captain! our fearful trip is done,
The ship has weather'd every rack, the prize we sought is
   won,
The port is near, the bells I hear, the people all exulting,
While follow eyes the steady keel, the vessel grim and
   daring;
      But O heart! heart! heart!
         O the bleeding drops of red,
            Where on the deck my Captain lies,
               Fallen cold and dead.

O Captain! my Captain! rise up and hear the bells;
Rise up – for you the flag is flung – for you the bugle trills,
For you bouquets and ribbon'd wreaths – for you the shores
   a-crowding,
For you they call, the swaying mass, their eager faces
   turning;
      Here Captain! dear father!
         This arm beneath your head!
            It is some dream that on the deck,
               You've fallen cold and dead.

My Captain does not answer, his lips are pale and still,
My father does not feel my arm, he has no pulse nor will,
The ship is anchor'd safe and sound, its voyage closed and
    done,
From fearful trip the victor ship comes in with object won:
    Exult O shores, and ring O bells!
        But I with mournful tread,
            Walk the deck my Captain lies,
                Fallen cold and dead.

Walt Whitman

Town Dog

I'm a town dog.
Usually I walk on a lead with my mistress;
I let children pat my head,
And politely use the gutter.
But sometimes,
Sometimes,
When it's
late
and dark
and shiny
and shadowy
and everyone is in bed,
I let myself out of the house
(Turning the key in my teeth),
Wearing my wolf's head
And my extra sharp fangs,
And I run and run
And have thrilling moonlit adventures.

And in the morning she says
'Tut-tut,
Who left the door open?'
and
'Tut-tut.
Look at that lazy dog. He needs more exercise!'

David Orme

One Old Oxford Ox

One old Oxford ox opening oysters,
Two teetotums totally tired trying to trot to Tadbury;
Three tall tigers tippling tuppenny tea;
Four fine foxes fanning fainting friars;
Five flighty flibbertigibbets foolishly fishing for flies;
Six sportsmen shooting snipes;
Seven Severn salmons swallowing shrimps;
Eight Englishmen eagerly examining Europe;
Nine nimble noblemen nibbling noodles;
Ten tinkers tinkling upon ten tin tinder-boxes with ten
    tenpenny tacks;
Eleven elephants elegantly equipt;
Twelve talkative tailors trimming tartan trousers.

Anon.

May

When Granny

Song-bird shut dem mout' an lissen,
Church bell don' bother to ring,
All de little stream keep quiet
When mi Granny sing.

De sun up in de sky get jealous,
Him wish him got her style,
For de whole place full o' brightness
When mi Granny smile.

First a happy soun' jus' bubblin'
From her belly, low an' sof',
Den a thunderclap o' merriment
When mi Granny laugh.

May

De tree branch dem all start swingin',
Puss an' dawg begin to prance,
Everyt'ing ketch de happy fever
When mi Granny dance.

All o' we look out fe Granny
Mek sure dat she satisfy,
For de whole worl' full o' sadness
When mi Granny cry.

Valerie Bloom

Slug

A 15-amp slug
you are likely to find
in the garden under a rock

Be careful
how you pick it up

You might get
a nasty shock.

Roger McGough

Rebekah

Rebekah, Rebekah,
Wake up from your sleep,
The cattle are thirsty
And so are the sheep
That come with the evening
Down from the high fell
To drink the sweet water
Of Paradise Well.

Rebekah, Rebekah,
The spring rises free
But the well it is locked
And you have the key,
And the sheep and the cattle,
Rebekah, are dry
And would drink of the water.
And so would I.

Charles Causley

Pomegranate
(for Chorlton Park School)

See, if it hadnie been for Persephone,
you'd have thought someone
was having you on
when you first clapped eyes on:
snow, a bald tree, yellow grass,
or happened to pass
a snowman in a field of frost,
or an icicle hanging from a sash-
windie, or bare roses, lashing sleet or slush.

You'd have never failed an exam,
because you simply wouldnie have gone
to school. You'd have had summer holidays
– a summer holiday symphony always –
if Persephone had clocked the Golden Rule,
and kept her beautiful lips sealed;
if she had not sucked those six small reds,
down in the deep dark world of the dead,
where every tree had lost its big head.

Next time someone offers you a wee bite of fruit –
think seriously for a second, then scoot.

Jackie Kay

The Lake Isle of Innisfree

I will arise and go now, and go to Innisfree,
And a small cabin build there, of clay and wattles made:
Nine bean-rows will I have there, a hive for the honey-bee,
And live alone in the bee-loud glade.

And I shall have some peace there, for peace comes
    dropping slow,
Dropping from the veils of the morning to where the cricket
    sings;
There midnight's all a glimmer, and noon a purple glow,
And evening full of the linnet's wings.

I will arise and go now, for always night and day
I hear lake water lapping with low sounds by the shore;
While I stand on the roadway, or on the pavements grey,
I hear it in the deep heart's core.

W.B. Yeats

Magpies

I saw eight magpies in a tree,
Two for you and six for me:
One for sorrow, two for mirth,
Three for a wedding, four for a birth;
Five for England, six for France,
Seven for a fiddler, eight for a dance.

Anon.

The Three Ravens

There were three ravens sat on a tree,
They were as black as they might be.

The one of them said to his make,
'Where shall we our breakfast take?'

'Down in yonder greenè field
There lies a knight slain under his shield;

'His hounds they lie down at his feet,
So well do they their master keep;

'His hawks they flie so eagerly,
There's no fowl dare come him nigh.

'Down there comes a fallow doe
As great with young as she might goe.

'She lift up his bloudy head
And kist his wounds that were so red.

'She gat him up upon her back
And carried him to earthen lake.

'She buried him before the prime,
She was dead herself ere evensong time.

'God send every gentleman
Such hounds, such hawks, and such a leman!'

Anon.

The Leader

I wanna be the leader
I wanna be the leader
Can I be the leader?
Can I? I can?
Promise? Promise?
Yippee, I'm the leader
I'm the leader

OK what shall we do?

Roger McGough

Fern Hill

Now as I was young and easy under the apple boughs
About the lilting house and happy as the grass was green,
 The night above the dingle starry,
  Time let me hail and climb
  Golden in the heydays of his eyes,
And honoured among wagons I was prince of the apple
 towns
And once below a time I lordly had the trees and leaves
  Trail with daisies and barley
  Down the rivers of the windfall light.

And as I was green and carefree, famous among the barns
About the happy yard and singing as the farm was home,
 In the sun that is young once only,
  Time let me play and be
  Golden in the mercy of his means,
And green and golden I was huntsman and herdsman, the
 calves
Sang to my horn, the foxes on the hills barked clear and cold.
  And the sabbath rang slowly
  In the pebbles of the holy streams.

All the sun long it was running, it was lovely, the hay
Fields high as the house, the tunes from the chimneys, it
   was air
   And playing, lovely and watery
      And fire green as grass.
   And nightly under the simple stars
As I rode to sleep the owls were bearing the farm away,
All the moon long I heard, blessed among stables, the
   nightjars
   Flying with the ricks, and the horses
      Flashing into the dark.

And then to awake, and the farm, like a wanderer white
With the dew, come back, the cock on his shoulder: it was all
      Shining, it was Adam and maiden,
         The sky gathered again
      And the sun grew round that very day.
So it must have been after the birth of the simple light
In the first, spinning place, the spellbound horses walking
   warm
      Out of the whinnying green stable
         On to the fields of praise.

May

And honoured among foxes and pheasants by the gay house
Under the new made clouds and happy as the heart was long,
    In the sun born over and over,
      I ran my heedless ways,
     My wishes raced through the house high hay
And nothing I cared, at my sky blue trades, that time allows
In all his tuneful turning so few and such morning songs
  Before the children green and golden
    Follow him out of grace,

Nothing I cared, in the lamb white days, that time would
  take me
Up to the swallow thronged loft by the shadow of my hand,
    In the moon that is always rising,
      Nor that riding to sleep
    I should hear him fly with the high fields
And wake to the farm forever fled from the childless land.
Oh as I was young and easy in the mercy of his means,
    Time held me green and dying
    Though I sang in my chains like the sea.

Dylan Thomas

Blue-Butterfly Day

It is blue-butterfly day here in spring,
And with these sky-flakes down in flurry on flurry
There is more unmixed colour on the wing
Than flowers will show for days unless they hurry.

But these flowers that fly and all but sing:
And now from having ridden out desire
They lie closed over in the wind and cling
Where wheels have freshly sliced the April mire.

Robert Frost

Just My Luck

'If weasels could fly,' said my Granny,
'I would give you four buckets of sweets,
Three mousetraps, two spoons and a tom-tom,
And lots more magnificent treats.'

'Then give me them now, quick!' I shouted
As a furry thing whizzed past my throat,
But she shook her head answering 'Sorry,
I said weasels, dear, that was a stoat.'

Richard Edwards

These I have Loved . . .

These I have loved:
      White plates and cups, clean-gleaming,
Ringed with blue lines; and feathery, faery dust;
Wet roofs, beneath the lamp-light; the strong crust
Of friendly bread; and many-tasting food;
Rainbows; and the blue bitter smoke of wood;
And radiant raindrops couching in cool flowers;
And flowers themselves, that sway through sunny hours,
Dreaming of moths that drink them under the moon;
Then, the cool kindliness of sheets, that soon
Smooth away trouble; and the rough male kiss
Of blankets; grainy wood; live hair that is
Shining and free; blue-massing clouds; the keen
Unpassioned beauty of a great machine;
The benison of hot water; furs to touch;
The good smell of old clothes; and other such –
The comfortable smell of friendly fingers,
Hair's fragrance, and the musty reek that lingers
About dead leaves and last year's ferns . . .

Dear names,
And thousand other throng to me! Royal flames;
Sweet water's dimpling laugh from tap or spring;
Holes in the ground; and voices that do sing;
Voices in laughter, too; and body's pain,
Soon turned to peace; and the deep-panting train;
Firm sands; the little dulling edge of foam
That browns and dwindles as the wave goes home;
And washen stones, gay for an hour; the cold
Graveness of iron; moist black earthen mould;
Sleep; and high places; footprints in the dew;
And oaks; and brown horse-chestnuts, glossy-new;
And new-peeled sticks; and shining pools on grass; –
All these have been my loves.

Rupert Brooke

Happiness

John had
Great Big
Waterproof
Boots on;
John had a
Great Big
Waterproof
Hat;
John had a
Great Big
Waterproof
Mackintosh –
And that
(Said John)
Is
That.

A.A. Milne

When Green Buds Hang

When green buds hang in the elm like dust
And sprinkle the lime like rain,
Forth I wander, forth I must,
And drink of life again.
Forth I must by hedgerow bowers
To look at the leaves uncurled,
And stand in the fields where cuckoo-flowers
Are lying about the world.

A.E. Housman

The Writer of this Poem

The writer of this poem
Is taller than a tree
As keen as the North wind
As handsome as can be

As bold as a boxing-glove
As sharp as a nib
As strong as scaffolding
As tricky as a fib

As smooth as a lolly-ice
As quick as a lick
As clean as a chemist-shop
As clever as a

The writer of this poem
Never ceases to amaze
He's one in a million billion
(Or so the poem says!)

Roger McGough

Mid-Term Break

I sat all morning in the college sick bay
Counting bells knelling classes to a close.
At two o'clock our neighbours drove me home.

In the porch I met my father crying –
He had always taken funerals in his stride –
And Big Jim Evans saying it was a hard blow.

The baby cooed and laughed and rocked the pram
When I came in, and I was embarrassed
By old men standing up to shake my hand

And tell me they were 'sorry for my trouble';
Whispers informed strangers I was the eldest,
Away at school, as my mother held my hand

In hers and coughed out angry tearless sighs.
At ten o'clock the ambulance arrived
With the corpse, stanched and bandaged by the nurses.

Next morning I went up into the room. Snowdrops
And candles soothed the bedside; I saw him
For the first time in six weeks. Paler now,

Wearing a poppy bruise on his left temple,
He lay in the four foot box as in his cot.
No gaudy scars, the bumper knocked him clear.

A four foot box, a foot for every year.

Seamus Heaney

A Cornish Charm

From Ghosties and Ghoulies
And long-leggity Beasties,
And all things that go BUMP
in the night –
Good Lord, deliver us!

Anon.

The Isle is Full of Noises

The isle is full of noises,
Sounds, and sweet airs, that give delight, and hurt not.
Sometimes a thousand twangling instruments
Will hum about mine ears; and sometimes voices,
That, if I then had wak'd after long sleep,
Will make me sleep again; and then, in dreaming,
The clouds methought would open and show riches
Ready to drop upon me; that, when I wak'd,
I cried to dream again.

William Shakespeare

Leisure

What is this life if, full of care,
We have no time to stand and stare.

No time to stand beneath the boughs
And stare as long as sheep or cows.

No time to see, when woods we pass,
Where squirrels hide their nuts in grass.

No time to see, in broad daylight,
Streams full of stars like skies at night.

No time to turn at Beauty's glance,
And watch her feet, how they can dance.

No time to wait till her mouth can
Enrich that smile her eyes began.

A poor life this if, full of care,
We have no time to stand and stare.

W.H. Davies

Close Cropped Hair

Close cropped hair feels good.
It should
It gives you street cred –
And, as I've always said,
It feels like having eyebrows
All over your head.

Linda Marshall

The Explosion

On the day of the explosion
Shadows pointed towards the pithead:
In the sun the slagheap slept.

May

Down the lane came men in pitboots
Coughing oath-edged talk and pipe-smoke,
Shouldering off the freshened silence.

One chased after rabbits; lost them;
Came back with a nest of lark's eggs;
Showed them; lodged them in the grasses.

So they passed in beards and moleskins,
Fathers, brothers, nicknames, laughter,
Through the tall gates standing open.

At noon, there came a tremor; cows
Stopped chewing for a second; sun,
Scarfed as in a heat-haze, dimmed.

The dead go on before us, they
Are sitting in God's house in comfort,
We shall see them face to face –

Plain as lettering in the chapels
It was said, and for a second
Wives saw men of the explosion

Larger than in life they managed –
Gold as on a coin, or walking
Somehow from the sun towards them,

One showing the eggs unbroken.

Philip Larkin

Magic

A web
captures the storm:
glass beads, safe in fine net,
gather sunlight as they sway
in high winds.

Judith Nicholls

Lauren

You're a new daisy
that's come up at night,
your skin is
a silk cover rubbed
against my hand.

You're a moon
drifting through frozen air,
the lady who helps me
when I'm hurt. You are
cream just whipped.

You're a red lipped flower,
the bit of butter
melting on my potato,
you're the hot water in my
bath, rushing around me.

You are god talking
quietly to horses,
a rainbow in the sky.
You're the moment
I get my sums right.

Barry Turrell

The Emergensea

The octopus awoke one morning and wondered what
    rhyme it was.
Looking at his alarm-clocktopus
he saw that it had stopped
and it was time to stop having a rest
and get himself dressed.
On every octofoot
he put an octosocktopus
but in his hurry, one foot got put
not into an octosock
but into an electric plug socket
and the octopus got a nasty electric shocktopus
and had to call the octodoctopus
who couldn't get in
to give any help or medicine
because the door was loctopus.
The octopus couldn't move, being in a state of
    octoshocktopus
so the octodoctopus bashed the door
to the floor
and the cure was as simple as could be:
a nice refreshing cup of seawater.

John Hegley

The Common and the Goose

The law locks up the man or woman
Who steals the goose from off the common
But leaves the greater felon loose
Who steals the common from the goose.

Anon.

The Older the Violin the Sweeter the Tune

Me Granny old
Me Granny wise
stories shine like a moon
from inside she eyes.

May

Me Granny can dance
Me Granny can sing
but she can't play violin.

Yet she always saying,
'Dih older dih violin
de sweeter de tune.'

Me Granny must be wiser
than the man inside the moon.

John Agard

Come unto these Yellow Sands

Come unto these yellow sands,
  And then take hands:
Court'sied when you have, and kissed,
  The wild waves whist, –
Foot it featly here and there;
And, sweet sprites, the burden bear.
    Hark, hark!
      Bow, wow,
    The watch-dogs bark:
      Bow, wow.
    Hark, hark! I hear
    The strain of strutting chanticleer
    Cry, Cock-a-diddle-dow!

William Shakespeare

Mobile Home for Sale

Judy is a delightful
Mobile Home
with Central Heating
a warm Basement
superb Penthouse views
and includes luxury
Deep Pile Carpets
in black and white.
Fully Air-Conditioned
by large wagging tail.
This Border collie
would suit large family of fleas.

Roger Stevens

One, Two, Buckle my Shoe

One, two,
Buckle my shoe;
Three, four,
Knock at the door;
Five, six,
Pick up sticks;
Seven, eight,
Lay them straight;
Nine, ten,
A big fat hen;
Eleven, twelve,
Dig and delve;
Thirteen, fourteen,
Maids a-courting;
Fifteen, sixteen,
Maids in the kitchen;
Seventeen, eighteen,
Maids in waiting;
Nineteen, twenty,
My plate's empty.

Anon.

30

The Farmer's Cat

Out in the fields
in Spring time,
the farmer's cat follows him
as he plants the seeds of corn.

> The cat dances with the rain drops
> and sleeps in the sun
> and when Autumn comes
> she sees that the farmer
> has a field full of corn.

Out in the fields
in Spring time,
the farmer's cat follows him
as he plants the peanut seeds.

> The cat dances with the rain drops
> and sleeps in the sun
> and when Autumn comes
> she sees that the farmer
> has a field of tasty peanuts.

Out in the fields
in Spring time,
the farmer watches while his cat
plants rows of tiny fish.

The cat dances with the rain drops
and sleeps in the sun
and dreams that when Autumn comes
she will fill her dish
with all the silver fish
that she's grown in the farmer's fields.

David Greygoose
after a translation by Xia Lu,
from the traditional Chinese

Small Wonders

Brand-new elephants roamed through the jungles.
Brand-new whales splashed down through the oceans.
God had slapped them together,
Happy as a kid making mud pies.

He wiped His hands clean.
'Now for the hard part,' He thought.
He took his workbench into the garden.
Delicately He placed in the bee's sting,
The moth's antenna,

His hand
Not trembling in the slightest.

Brian Patten

June

Summer

Winter is cold-hearted,
  Spring is yea and nay,
Autumn is a weathercock
  Blown every way:
Summer days for me
When every leaf is on the tree;

When Robin's not a beggar,
  And Jenny Wren's a bride,
And larks hang singing, singing, singing,
  Over the wheatfields wide,
  And anchored lilies ride,
And the pendulum spider
  Swings from side to side,

And blue-black beetles transact business,
   And gnats fly in a host,
And furry caterpillars hasten
   That no time be lost,
And moths grow fat and thrive,
And ladybirds arrive.

Before green apples blush,
   Before green nuts embrown,
Why, one day in the country
   Is worth a month in town;
   Is worth a day and a year
Of the dusty, musty, lag-last fashion
   That days drone elsewhere.

Christina Rossetti

2

The Hyena

The hyena has neither charm nor wit.
Beauty and courage? He hasn't a bit,
In the animal world he has no clout,
So I don't know what he's laughing about.

Valerie Bloom

Summer Dawn

Pray but one prayer for me 'twixt thy closed lips,
Think but one thought of me up in the stars.
The summer night waneth, the morning light slips
    Faint and gray 'twixt the leaves of the aspen, betwixt the
    cloud-bars,
That are patiently waiting there for the dawn:
    Patient and colourless, though Heaven's gold
Waits to float through them along with the sun.
Far out in the meadows, above the young corn,
    The heavy elms wait, and restless and cold
The uneasy wind rises; the roses are dun;
Through the long twilight they pray for the dawn
Round the lone house in the midst of the corn.
        Speak but one word to me over the corn,
        Over the tender, bow'd locks of the corn.

William Morris

Down Jericho Way

Yesterday at 4.00
    I saved a worm
    laying in the road.

Picked it up
Threw it in a garden
Number fifty-one.

It was not a fire worm
    a rare worm
a worm with a crown on its head.

It was not a glow worm
    a slow worm
    silver
    or golden
    or pied.

Just an ordinary worm
Dying itself in the sun.

Down Jericho Way.

Peter Dixon

To Make a Prairie

To make a prairie it takes a clover and one bee,
One clover, and a bee,
And revery.
The revery alone will do,
If bees are few.

Emily Dickinson

The Trial of Derek Drew

The charges

Derek Drew:
For leaving his reading book at home.
For scribbling his handwriting practice.
For swinging on the pegs in the cloakroom.
For sabotaging the girls' skipping.
For doing disgusting things with his dinner.

Also charged

Mrs Alice Drew (née Alice Jukes):
For giving birth to Derek Drew.
Mr Dennis Drew:
For aiding and abetting Mrs Drew.
Mrs Muriel Drew and Mr Donald Drew:
For giving birth to Dennis Drew, etc.
Mrs Jane Jukes and Mr Paul Jukes:
For giving birth to Alice Jukes, etc.
Previous generations of the Drew and Jukes families:
For being born, etc., etc.

Witnesses

'He's *always* forgetting his book.' Mrs Pine.
'He *can* write neatly, if he wants to.' Ditto.
'I seen him on the pegs, Miss!'
'And me!' 'And me!' Friends of the accused.
'He just kept jumpin' in the rope!' Eight third-year girls
In Miss Hodge's class.
'It was disgusting!' Mrs Foot (dinner-lady).

For the defence

'I was never *in* the cloakroom!' Derek Drew.

Mitigating circumstances

This boy is ten years old.
He asks for 386 other charges to be taken into
  consideration.
'He's not like this at home,' his mother says.

The verdict

Guilty.

The sentence

Life!
And do his handwriting again.

Allan Ahlberg

Evening: Ponte al Mare, Pisa

The sun is set; the swallows are asleep;
　　The bats are flitting fast in the grey air;
The slow soft toads out of damp corners creep,
　　And evening's breath, wandering here and there
Over the quivering surface of the stream,
Wakes not one ripple from its summer dream.

There is no dew on the dry grass tonight,
　　Nor damp within the shadow of the trees;
The wind is intermitting, dry, and light;
　　And in the inconstant motion of the breeze
The dust and straws are driven up and down,
And whirled about the pavement of the town.

Within the surface of the fleeting river
　　The wrinkled image of the city lay,
Immovably unquiet, and for ever
It trembles, but it never fades away . . .

Percy Bysshe Shelley

This is Just to Say

This is just to say
I have eaten
the plums
that were in
the icebox

and which
you were probably
saving
for breakfast

Forgive me
they were delicious
so sweet
and so cold

William Carlos Williams

Class Discussion

'In the class discussion, Jane, you hardly said a word.
We all aired our opinions but from you we rarely heard.
You sat and stared in silence surrounded by the chatter,
Now tell me, Jane, and please be plain,
Is there anything the matter?'

Jane looked up and then she spoke,
Her voice was clear and low:
'There are many people in this world
Who are rather quiet you know!'

Gervase Phinn

Noon

The midday hour of twelve the clock counts o'er,
  A sultry stillness lulls the air asleep;
The very buzz of flies is heard no more,
  Nor faintest wrinkles o'er the waters creep.
Like one large sheet of glass the pool does shine,
  Reflecting in its face the burnt sunbeam:
The very fish their sturting play decline,
  Seeking the willow shadows 'side the stream.
And, where the hawthorn branches o'er the pool,
  The little bird, forsaking song and nest,
Flutters on dripping twigs his limbs to cool,
  And splashes in the stream his burning breast.
Oh, free from thunder, for a sudden shower,
  To cherish nature in this noonday hour!

John Clare

Auntie Betty Thinks She's Batgirl

Auntie Betty pulls her cloak on
And the mask – the one with ears.
Almost ready, check the lipstick,
Wait until the neighbours cheer.
Through the window. What a leap!
She lands right in the driver's seat.
Off she goes with style and grace
To make our world a better place.

Andrea Shavick

I Believe

I believe,
I believe in the sun
even when it is not shining.
I believe in love
even when I cannot feel it.
I believe in God
even when God is silent.

Anon.
Found in a Jewish hiding place during the Holocaust

The Sounds in the Evening

The sounds in the evening
Go all through the house,
The click of the clock
And the pick of the mouse,
The footsteps of people
Upon the top floor,
The skirts of my mother
That brush by my door,
The crick in the boards,
And the creak of the chairs,
The fluttering murmurs
Outside on the stairs,
The ring at the bell,
The arrival of guests,
The laugh of my father
At one of his jests,
The clashing of dishes
As dinner goes in,
The babble of voices
That distance makes thin,
The mewings of cats
That seem just by my ear,
The hooting of owls

That can never seem near,
The queer little noises
That no one explains –
Till the moon through the slats
Of my window-blind rains,
And the world of my eyes
And my ears melts like steam
As I find in my pillow
The world of my dream.

Eleanor Farjeon

The Cod

There's something very strange and odd
About the habits of the Cod.

For when you're swimming in the sea,
He sometimes bites you on the knee.

And though his bites are not past healing,
It is a most unpleasant feeling.

And when you're diving down below,
He often nips you on the toe.

And though he doesn't hurt you much,
He has a disagreeable touch.

There's one thing to be said for him, –
It is a treat to see him swim.

But though he swims in graceful curves,
He rather gets upon your nerves.

Lord Alfred Douglas

natural high

my mother is a
red
woman

she
gets high
on clean children

grows
common sense

injects
tales
with heroines

fumes
over dirty habits

hits the sky
on bad lines

cracking meteors

my mother
gets red
with the sun

Jean Binta Breeze

Shell

Said a mother crab to her daughter,
'Look, that's Brighton Pier,
So pick up that shell my darling
And tell me what you hear.'

The babe picked up the shining shell
Off the gritty sand
And placing it carefully to her ear said,
'I can hear the land.'

Gareth Owen

In the Summer

In the summer when I go to bed
The sun still streaming overhead
My bed becomes so small and hot
With sheets and pillow in a knot,
And then I lie and try to see
The things I'd really like to be.

I think I'd be a glossy cat
A little plump, but not too fat.
I'd never touch a bird or mouse
I'm much too busy round the house.

And then a fierce and hungry hound
The king of dogs for miles around;
I'd chase the postman just for fun
To see how quickly he could run.

Perhaps I'd be a crocodile
Within the marshes of the Nile
And paddle in the river-bed
With dripping mud-caps on my head.

Or maybe next a mountain goat
With shaggy whiskers at my throat,
Leaping streams and jumping rocks
In stripey pink and purple socks.

Or else I'd be a polar bear
And on an iceberg make my lair;
I'd keep a shop in Baffin Sound
To sell icebergs by the pound.

And then I'd be a wise old frog
Squatting on a sunken log,
I'd teach the fishes lots of games
And how to read and write their names.

An Indian lion then I'd be
And lounge about on my settee;
I'd feed on nothing but bananas
And spend all day in my pyjamas.

I'd like to be a tall giraffe
Making lots of people laugh,
I'd do a tap-dance in the street
With little bells upon my feet.

And then I'd be a foxy fox
Streaking through the hollyhocks,
Horse or hound would ne'er catch me
I'm a master of disguise, you see.

I think I'd be a chimpanzee
With musical ability,
I'd play a silver clarinet
Or form a Monkey String Quartet.

And then a snake with scales of gold
Guarding hoards of wealth untold,
No thief would dare to steal a pin –
But friends of mine I would let in.

But then before I really know
Just what I'd be or where I'd go
My bed becomes so wide and deep
And all my thoughts are fast asleep.

Thomas Hood

Cousin Nell

Cousin Nell
married a frogman
in the hope
that one day
he would turn into
a handsome prince.

Instead he turned into
a sewage pipe
near Gravesend
and was never seen again.

Roger McGough

She Walks in Beauty

She walks in beauty, like the night
Of cloudless climes and starry skies,
And all that's best of dark and bright
Meets in her aspect and her eyes,
Thus mellow'd to that tender light
Which heaven to gaudy day denies.

One shade the more, one ray the less
Had half impair'd the nameless grace
Which waves in every raven tress
Or softly lightens o'er her face,
Where thoughts serenely sweet express
How pure, how dear their dwelling-place.

And on that cheek and o'er that brow
So soft, so calm, yet eloquent,
The smiles that win, the tints that glow
But tell of days in goodness spent, –
A mind at peace with all below,
A heart whose love is innocent.

Lord Byron

Binsey Poplars
felled 1879

My aspens dear, whose airy cages quelled,
Quelled or quenched in leaves the leaping sun,
All felled, felled, are all felled;
   Of a fresh and following folded rank
        Not spared, not one
        That dandled a sandalled
     Shadow that swam or sank
On meadow and river and wind-wandering weed-winding
   bank.

O if we but knew what we do
      When we delve or hew –
Hack and rack the growing green!
     Since country is so tender
To touch, her being so slender,
That, like this sleek and seeing ball
But a prick will make no eye at all,

Where we, even where we mean
    To mend her we end her,
  When we hew or delve:
After-comers cannot guess the beauty been.
  Ten or twelve, only ten or twelve
    Strokes of havoc unselve
      The sweet especial scene,
    Rural scene, a rural scene,
    Sweet especial rural scene.

Gerard Manley Hopkins

My Parakeet

Anyone see my parakeet, Skeet?
He's small and neat,
He's really sweet,
with his pick-pick beak,
And his turn-back feet.

Skeet, Skeet, I wouldn't tell a lie
You are the green-pearl of my eye.

Grace Nichols

Judith

Judith, why are you kneeling on the lawn
With your ear against that little weed? What are you
   listening for?
Hush, says Judith, go away and leave me,
I'm waiting for this dandelion to roar.

Judith, why are you sitting in the wood
With your eyes fixed on your wristwatch? Do you want to
   know the time?
Hush, says Judith, go away and leave me,
I want to hear the bluebells when they chime.

Judith, why are you standing by that tree
With your handkerchief out ready? Come inside and go to
   sleep.
Hush, says Judith, go away and leave me,
I'm waiting for this willow tree to weep.

Judith, why are you lying in your bed
With some hay stalks in your left hand and some oatflakes
   in your right?
Hush, says Judith, go away and leave me,
A nightmare may come visiting tonight.

Richard Edwards

A Smuggler's Song

If you wake at midnight and hear a horse's feet,
Don't go drawing back the blind, or looking in the street,

Them that asks no questions isn't told a lie.
Watch the wall, my darling, while the Gentlemen go by!
      Five and twenty ponies,
      Trotting through the dark –
      Brandy for the Parson,
      Baccy for the Clerk;
      Laces for a lady; letters for a spy,
And watch the wall, my darling, while the Gentlemen go by!

Running round the woodlump if you chance to find
Little barrels, roped and tarred, all full of brandy-wine;
Don't you shout to come and look, nor take 'em for your
    play;
Put the brushwood back again, – and they'll be gone next
    day!

If you see the stableyard setting open wide;
If you see a tired horse lying down inside;
If your mother mends a coat cut about and tore;
If the lining's wet and warm – don't you ask no more!

If you meet King George's men, dressed in blue and red,
You be careful what you say, and mindful what is said.
If they call you 'pretty maid', and chuck you 'neath the chin,
Don't you tell where no one is, nor yet where no one's been!

Knocks and footsteps round the house – whistles after dark –
You've no call for running out till the housedogs bark.
Trusty's here and Pincher's here, and see how dumb they lie –
They don't fret to follow when the Gentlemen go by!

If you do as you've been told, likely there's a chance,
You'll be given a dainty dolly, – all the way from France,
With a cap of Valenciennes, and a velvet hood –
A present from the Gentlemen, along o' being good!
      Five and twenty ponies,
      Trotting through the dark –
      Brandy for the Parson,
      Baccy for the Clerk;
Them that asks no questions isn't told a lie –
Watch the wall, my darling, while the Gentlemen go by!

Rudyard Kipling

A Chance in France

'Stay at home,'
Mum said.

But I –
took a chance
in France,
turned grey
for the day
in St Tropez,
I forgot
what I did
in Madrid,
had some tussles
in Brussels
with a trio
from Rio,
lost my way
in Bombay,
nothing wrong
in Hong Kong,
felt calmer
in Palma,
and quite nice
in Nice,

yes, felt finer
in China,
took a room
in Khartoum
and a villa
in Manilla,
had a 'do'
in Peru
with a llama
from Lima,
took a walk
in New York
with a man
from Milan,
lost a sneaker
in Costa Rica,
got lumbago
in Tobago,
felt a menace
in Venice,
was a bore
in Singapore,
lost an ear
in Korea,
some weight
in Kuwait,
tried my best
as a guest
in old Bucharest,

got the fleas
in Belize
and came home.

Pie Corbett

Choosing their Names

Our old cat has kittens three –
What do you think their names should be?

One is a tabby, with emerald eyes,
   And a tail that's long and slender,
And into a temper she quickly flies
   If you ever by chance offend her:
      I think we shall call her this –
      I think we shall call her that –
Now, don't you think that Pepperpot
   Is a nice name for a cat?

One is black, with a frill of white,
    And her feet are all white fur, too;
If you stroke her she carries her tail upright
    And quickly begins to purr, too!
        I think we shall call her this –
        I think we shall call her that –
Now don't you think that Sootikin
    Is a nice name for a cat?

One is a tortoise-shell, yellow and black,
    With plenty of white about him;
If you tease him, at once he sets up his back:
    He's a quarrelsome one, ne'er doubt him.
        I think we shall call him this –
        I think we shall call him that –
Now don't you think that Scratchaway
    Is a nice name for a cat?

Our old cat has kittens three
And I fancy these their names will be;
Pepperpot, Sootikin, Scratchaway – there!
Were ever kittens with these to compare?
And we call the old mother –
            Now, what do you think?
Tabitha Longclaws Tiddley Wink.

Thomas Hood

Classroom Helper

Can we borrow your chipmunk, Miss?
He's such a useful pet,
So tidy and efficient,
Our best pencil sharpener yet!

Sue Cowling

When I Set Out for Lyonnesse

When I set out for Lyonnesse,
    A hundred miles away,
    The rime was on the spray,
And starlight lit my lonesomeness
When I set out for Lyonnesse
    A hundred miles away.

What should bechance at Lyonnesse
    While I should sojourn there
    No prophet durst declare,
Nor did the wisest wizard guess
What would bechance at Lyonnesse
    While I should sojourn there.

When I came back from Lyonnesse
    With magic in my eyes,
    All marked with mute surmise
My radiance rare and fathomless,
When I came back from Lyonnesse
    With magic in my eyes!

Thomas Hardy

On a Blue Day

On a blue day
when the brown heat
scorches the grass
and stings my legs with sweat

I go running like a fool
up the hill towards the trees
and my heart beats loudly
like a kettle boiling dry.

I need a bucket the size of the sky
filled with cool, cascading water.

At evening
the cool air rubs my back
I listen to the bees
working for their honey

and the sunset pours light
over my head like a waterfall.

David Harmer

Changed

For months he taught us, stiff-faced.
His old tweed jacket closely buttoned up,
his gestures careful and deliberate.

We didn't understand what he was teaching us.
It was as if a veil, a gauzy bandage, got between
what he was showing us and what we thought we saw.

He had the air of a gardener, fussily protective
of young seedlings, but we couldn't tell
if he was hiding something or we simply couldn't see it.

At first we noticed there were often scraps of leaves
on the floor where he had stood. Later, thin wisps
of thread like spider's web fell from his jacket.

Finally we grew to understand the work. And on that day
he opened his jacket, which to our surprise
seemed lined with patterned fabric of many shimmering hues.

Then he smiled and sighed. And with this movement
the lining rippled and instantly the room was filled
with a flickering storm of swirling butterflies.

Dave Calder

The Bookworm

'I'm tired – Oh, tired of books,' said Jack,
  'I long for meadows green,
And woods where shadowy violets
  Nod their cool leaves between;
I long to see the ploughman's stride
  His darkening acres o'er,
To hear the hoarse sea-waters drive
  Their billows 'gainst the shore;
I long to watch the sea-mew wheel
  Back to her rock-perched mate;
Or, where the breathing cows are housed,
  Lean, dreaming at the gate.
Something has gone, and ink and print
  Will never bring it back;
I long for the green fields again,
  I'm tired of books,' said Jack.

Walter de la Mare

July

Cat Kisses

Sandpaper kisses
on a cheek or a chin –
that is the way
for a day to begin!

Sandpaper kisses –
a cuddle, a purr.
I have an alarm clock
that's covered with fur.

Bobbi Katz

Little Silver Aeroplane

Little silver aeroplane
Up in the sky,
Where are you going to
Flying so high?
Over the mountains
Over the sea
Little silver aeroplane
Please take me.

Anon.

Cock-Crow

Out of the wood of thoughts that grows by night
To be cut down by the sharp axe of light –
Out of the night, two cocks together crow,
Cleaving the darkness with a silver blow:
And bright before my eyes twin trumpeters stand,
Heralds of splendour, one at either hand,
Each facing each as in a coat of arms:
The milkers lace their boots up at the farms.

Edward Thomas

Battle Hymn of the American Republic

Mine eyes have seen the glory of the coming of the Lord;
He is trampling out the vintage where the grapes of wrath
  are stored;
He hath loosed the fatal lightning of his terrible swift sword:
  His Truth is marching on.

I have seen him in the watch-fires of a hundred circling
  camps;
They have builded him an altar in the evening dews and
  damps;
I have read his righteous sentence by the dim and flaring
  lamps:
  His Day is marching on.

I have read a fiery gospel, writ in burnished rows of steel:
'As you deal with my contemners, so you with my grace
  shall deal';
Let the Hero born of woman crush the serpent with his heel,
  Since God is marching on.

He has sounded forth the trumpet that shall never call
    retreat;
He is sifting out the hearts of men before his judgment-seat;
O be swift, my soul, to answer him; be jubilant, my feet!
    Our God is marching on.

In the beauty of the lilies Christ was born across the sea,
With a glory in his bosom that transfigures you and me;
As he died to make men holy, let us die to make men free,
    While God is marching on.

He is coming like the glory of the morning on the wave;
He is wisdom to the mighty, he is succour to the brave;
So the world shall be his footstool, and the soul of time his
    slave;
    Our God is marching on.

Julia Ward Howe

Grandad's Garden

is heady with perfumes,
wallflowers, carnations,
velvet roses, lilac.

All the bees get tipsy.

He wins prizes. There are
cups, shields around the clock
on the sideboard.

Grandma polishes them
with yellow dusters.

Grandad shows his garden to me
every Sunday. Sweet peas
like bright butterflies,
sky-blue scabious,
the fairy hats of columbines.

His garden is a place
(listen to those ring-a-ding
Canterbury bells!)
that's telling you

what wonderful things
love can do.

Matt Simpson

If You

If you,
Like me,
Were made of fur
And sun warmed you,
Like me,
You'd purr.

Karla Kuskin

231

The River

The River's a wanderer,
A nomad, a tramp,
He never chooses one place
To set up his camp.

The River's a winder,
Through valley and hill
He twists and he turns,
He just cannot be still.

The River's a hoarder
And he buries down deep
Those little treasures
That he wants to keep.

The River's a baby,
He gurgles and hums,
And sounds like he's happily
Sucking his thumbs.

The River's a singer,
As he dances along,
The countryside echoes
The notes of his song.

The River's a monster,
Hungry and vexed,
He's gobbled up trees
And he'll swallow you next.

Valerie Bloom

Children with Adults

My auntie gives me a colouring book and crayons.
I begin to colour.
After a while she looks over to see what I have done and
　　says
you've gone over the lines
that's what you've done.
What do you think they're there for, ay?
Some kind of statement is it?
Going to be a rebel are we?
I begin to cry.
My uncle gives me a hanky and some blank paper
do your own designs he says
I begin to colour.
When I have done he looks over and tells me they are all
　　very good.
He is lying,
only some of them are.

John Hegley

The Poplar Field

The poplars are felled, farewell to the shade
And the whispering sound of the cool colonnade,
The winds play no longer, and sing in the leaves,
Nor Ouse on his bosom their image receives.

Twelve years have elapsed since I last took a view
Of my favourite field and the bank where they grew,
And now in the grass behold they are laid,
And the tree is my seat that once lent me a shade.

The blackbird has fled to another retreat
Where the hazels afford him a screen from the heat,
And the scene where his melody charmed me before,
Resounds with his sweet-flowing ditty no more.

My fugitive years are all hasting away,
And I must ere long lie as lowly as they,
With a turf on my breast, and a stone at my head,
Ere another such grove shall arise in its stead.

'Tis a sight to engage me, if any thing can,
To muse on the perishing pleasures of man;
Though his life be a dream, his enjoyments, I see,
Having a being less durable even than he.

William Cowper

The Poem

It is only a little twig
With a green bud at the end;
But if you plant it,
And water it,
And set it where the sun will be above it,
It will grow into a tall bush,
With many flowers,
And leaves which thrust hither and thither
Sparkling.
From its roots will come freshness,
And beneath it the grass-blades
Will bend and recover themselves,
And clash one upon another
In the blowing wind.

But if you take my twig
And throw it into a closet
With mousetraps and blunted tools,
It will shrivel and waste.
And, some day,
When you open the door,
You will think it an old twisted nail,
And sweep it into the dust bin
With other rubbish.

Amy Lowell

Not Waving but Drowning

Nobody heard him, the dead man,
But still he lay moaning:
I was much further out than you thought
And not waving but drowning.

Poor chap, he always loved larking
And now he's dead
It must have been too cold for him his heart gave way,
They said.

Oh, no no no, it was too cold always
(Still the dead one lay moaning)
I was much too far out all my life
And not waving but drowning.

Stevie Smith

The Eel

I don't mind eels
Except as meals.
And the way they feels.

Ogden Nash

Early in the Morning

Early in the morning
The water hits the rocks,
The birds are making noises
Like old alarum clocks,
The soldier on the skyline
Fires a golden gun
And over the back of the chimney-stack
Explodes the silent sun.

Charles Causley

A Spike of Green

When I went out
The sun was hot,
It shone upon
My flower pot.

And there I saw
A spike of green
That no one else
Had ever seen!

On other days
The things I see
Are mostly old
Except for me.

But this green spike
So new and small
Had never yet
Been seen at all!

Barbara Baker

Self-Pity

I never saw a wild thing
sorry for itself.
A small bird will drop frozen dead from a bough
without ever having felt sorry for itself.

D.H. Lawrence

When my Friend Anita Runs

When my friend Anita runs
she runs straight into the headalong –
legs flashing over grass, daisies, mounds.

When my friend Anita runs
she sticks out her chest like an Olympic
champion – face all serious concentration.

And you'll never catch her looking around,
until she flies into the invisible tape
that says, she's won.

Then she turns to give me
this big grin and hug.

O to be able to run like Anita
run like Anita,
who runs like a cheetah.
If only, just for once, I could beat her.

Grace Nichols

Sun Hat

Oh, what a sweet child is Hannah Hyde,
Oh, how thoughtful, oh, how nice,
To buy a hat with a brim so wide,
It gives shade to the frogs
And the worms and the mice.

Shel Silverstein

Everyone Sang

Everyone suddenly burst out singing;
And I was filled with such delight
As prisoned birds must find in freedom
Winging wildly across the white
Orchards and dark-green fields; on; on; and out of sight.

Everyone's voice was suddenly lifted,
And beauty came like the setting sun.
My heart was shaken with tears; and horror
Drifted away . . . O but every one
Was a bird; and the song was wordless; the singing will
   never be done.

Siegfried Sassoon

Bed in Summer

In winter I get up at night
And dress by yellow candle-light.
In summer, quite the other way,
I have to go to bed by day.

I have to go to bed and see
The birds still hopping on the tree,
Or hear the grown-up people's feet
Still going past me in the street.

And does it not seem hard to you,
When all the sky is clear and blue,
And I should like so much to play,
To have to go to bed by day?

Robert Louis Stevenson

20

The Song of Arabella Jellyfish

I'm Arabella Jellyfish,
Star of stage and tellyfish.
I'm not a finned or shellyfish
Or some exotic delifish,
Or an ugly smellyfish,
But more a bright
Intelli-type of
Floaty, floaty
By the boaty,
Flimsy whimsy
Airy fairy,
Iddelli, diddleli
Terriby fiddleli
Delica-jellicafish.

Ernest Henry

Salestalk

She sells seashells on the seashore.
I've heard it before.

Well, he sells red leather weatherproofs
on the shop floor.
Nah! That's a bore.

Well, I hear tell
that she sells selfish shellfish
from the top shelf of the shelter
by the chip-shop door.
Hmm. Tell me more.

Well, let me just yell
that we sell swell yellow lollies
from red lorries
and big red brollies
from mellow yellow lorries,
the brollies
all wrapped
rapidly
in big bright boxes of straw,

and the lollies
all linked loosely
in bunches of four.
Cor! . . . (What for?)

Tony Mitton

The Eagle

He clasps the crag with crooked hands;
Close to the sun in lonely lands,
Ringed with the azure world, he stands.

The wrinkled sea beneath him crawls;
He watches from his mountain walls,
And like a thunderbolt he falls.

Alfred Lord Tennyson

Foxgloves

Foxgloves on the moon keep to dark caves.
They come out at the dark of the moon only and in waves
Swarm through the moon-towns and wherever there's a
　chink
Slip into the houses and spill all the money, clink-clink,
And crumple the notes and re-arrange the silver dishes,
And dip hands into the goldfish bowls and stir the
　goldfishes,
And thumb the edges of the mirrors, and touch the sleepers
Then at once vanish into the far distance with a wild laugh
　leaving the house smelling faintly of Virginia Creepers.

Ted Hughes

My Cat

My cat
got fatter
and fatter.
I didn't know
what was the matter.
Then,
know what she did?
She went into the cupboard
and hid.

She was fat when she went in,
but she came out
thin.
I had a peep.
Know what I saw?
Little kittens
all in a heap
– 1 – 2 – 3 – 4.

My cat's great.

Nigel Gray

Postcard Poem: Solo

Mum, you needn't have worried one bit.
I travelled fine, fine, solo. Carried
in steelbird-belly of music shows.
I ate two passengers' pudding twice.
Nibbled nothings nutty and chocolatey.
Sipped cool Cokes. Had more nibbles.
All over mountain after mountain.
Over different oceans. Over
weird clouds, like snow hills
with trails of straggly shapes
drifting, searching. And strangers
talked – Germans going on big-fish hunt,
Italians to ride glass-bottomed boat,
a Dane to do snorkelling. Then, Mum,
I hopped from steelbird-belly, among
sun-roasted people of a palmtree place.
Welcome to Jamaica, voices called out.
Whole family hugged a sweating me
and took me off. Other exotics
got collected up in cars and coaches
to be naked on beaches, while
steelbird stood there shining-ready
for more come-and-go migrations.

James Berry

Instructions for Giants

Please do not step on swing parks, youth clubs,
  cinemas or discos.
Please flatten all schools!

Please do not eat children, pop stars, TV soap actors,
  kind grannies who give us 50p.
Please feel free to gobble up dentists and teachers
  any time you like!

Please do not block out the sunshine.
Please push all rain clouds over to France.

Please do not drink the public swimming pool.
Please eat all cabbage fields, vegetable plots
  and anything green that grows in the
    boring countryside!

Please do not trample kittens, lambs or other baby animals.
Please take spiders and snakes, ants and beetles home for
  your own pets.

Please stand clear of jets passing.
Please sew up the ozone layer.
Please mind where you're putting your big feet –
and no sneaking off to China when we're playing
hide-and-seek!

John Rice

Fantasia

I dream
of
giving birth
to
a child
who will ask,
'Mother,
what was war?'

Eve Merriam

The Hippopotamus Song

A bold Hippopotamus was standing one day
On the banks of the cool Shalimar.
He gazed at the bottom as it peacefully lay
By the light of the evening star.
Away on a hilltop sat combing her hair
His fair Hippopotamine maid;
The Hippopotamus was no ignoramus
And sang her this sweet serenade.

   Mud, Mud, glorious mud,
   Nothing quite like it for cooling the blood!
   So follow me, follow,
   Down to the hollow
   And there let us wallow
   In glorious mud!

The fair Hippopotama he aimed to entice
From her seat on that hilltop above,
As she hadn't got a ma to give her advice,
Came tiptoeing down to her love.
Like thunder the forest re-echoed the sound
Of the song that they sang as they met.
His inamorata adjusted her garter
And lifted her voice in duet.

Mud, Mud, glorious mud,
Nothing quite like it for cooling the blood!
So follow me, follow,
Down to the hollow
And there let us wallow
In glorious mud!

Now more Hippopotami began to convene
On the banks of that river so wide.
I wonder now what am I to say of the scene
That ensued by the Shalimar side?
They dived all at once with an ear-splitting splosh
Then rose to the surface again,
A regular army of Hippopotami
All singing this haunting refrain.

Mud! Mud! Glorious mud!
Nothing quite like it for cooling the blood.
So follow me, follow,
Down to the hollow
And there let us wallow
In glorious mud!

Michael Flanders

Triolet

I wish I were a jellyfish
That cannot fall downstairs:
Of all the things I wish to wish
I wish I were a jellyfish
That hasn't any cares,
And doesn't even have to wish
'I wish I were a jellyfish
That cannot fall downstairs.'

G.K. Chesterton

So We'll Go No More a-Roving

So we'll go no more a-roving
    So late into the night,
Though the heart be still as loving,
    And the moon be still as bright.

For the sword outwears its sheath,
    And the soul outwears the breast,
And the heart must pause to breathe,
    And love itself have rest.

Though the night was made for loving,
    And the day returns too soon,
Yet we'll go no more a-roving
    By the light of the moon.

Lord Byron

Mocking Bird

Hush, little baby, don't say a word,
Papa's going to buy you a mocking bird.

If the mocking bird won't sing,
Papa's going to buy you a diamond ring.

If the diamond ring turns to brass,
Papa's going to buy you a looking-glass.

If the looking-glass gets broke,
Papa's going to buy you a billy-goat.

If that billy-goat runs away,
Papa's going to buy you another today.

Anon.

August

At Home, Abroad

All summer
I dream of
places I've never
been
where I might
see faces
I've never seen,
like the dark
face of my
father in
Nigeria,
or the pale
face of my mother in
the Highlands,
or the bright
faces of my
cousins at Land's End.

All summer
I spell the names
of tricky countries
just in case
I get a sudden
invite: Madagascar,
Cameroon. I draw
cartoons of
airports, big and small.
Who will meet me?
Will they
shake hands or
kiss both cheeks?
I draw
duty-frees
with every
country's favourite
sweetie, smiling
a sugary welcome,
and myself,
cap-peaked,
wondering if I am
'home'.

Jackie Kay

The Moon

The moon was but a chin of gold
A night or two ago,
And now she turns her perfect face
Upon the world below.

Emily Dickinson

A Fairy went a-Marketing

A fairy went a-marketing –
  She bought a little fish;
She put it in a crystal bowl
  Upon a golden dish.
An hour she sat in wonderment
  And watched its silver gleam,
And then she gently took it up
  And slipped it in a stream.

A fairy went a-marketing –
  She bought a coloured bird;
It sang the sweetest, shrillest song
  That ever she had heard.
She sat beside its painted cage
  And listened half the day,
And then she opened wide the door
  And let it fly away.

A fairy went a-marketing –
  She bought a winter gown
All stitched about with gossamer
  And lined with thistledown.
She wore it all the afternoon
  With prancing and delight,
Then gave it to a little frog
  To keep him warm at night.

A fairy went a-marketing –
  She bought a gentle mouse
To take her tiny messages,
  To keep her tiny house.
All day she kept its busy feet
  Pit-patting to and fro,
And then she kissed its silken ears,
  Thanked it, and let it go.

Rose Fyleman

She Sells Sea-Shells

She sells sea-shells on the sea shore;
The shells that she sells are sea-shells I'm sure.
So if she sells sea-shells on the sea shore,
I'm sure that the shells are sea-shore shells.

Anon.

The Swing

How do you like to go up in a swing,
   Up in the air so blue?
Oh, I do think it the pleasantest thing
   Ever a child can do!

Up in the air and over the wall,
    Till I can see so wide,
Rivers and trees and cattle and all
    Over the countryside –

Till I look down on the garden green,
    Down on the roof so brown –
Up in the air I go flying again,
    Up in the air and down!

                              Robert Louis Stevenson

Lost Garden

There's a scareghost in the car park
and I've seen him quite a lot
His head is half a cabbage
and his nose a big shallot.

He haunts in parks of diesel fume
his head towards the stars
– in a world that's made of tarmac
in a world that's built for cars.

He walks where once his garden grew
his pumpkins by the wall
lavender and larkspur
– the evening songbird's call.

He seeks the scent of roseflower
he sighs for yesteryears
With a head that's half a cabbage
and a face that's made of tears.

Peter Dixon

The Invisible Man

The invisible man is a joker
Who wears an invisible grin
And the usual kind of visible clothes
Which cover up most of him,

But there's nothing above his collar
Or at the end of his sleeves,
And his laughter is like the invisible wind
Which rustles the visible leaves.

When the visible storm clouds gather
He strides through the visible rain
In a special invisible see-through cloak
Then invisibly back again.

But he wears a thick, visible overcoat
To go out when it visibly snows
And the usual visible footprints
Get left wherever he goes.

In the visible heat-haze of summer
And the glare of the visible sun,
He undoes his visible buttons
With invisible fingers and thumb,

Takes off his visible jacket,
Loosens his visible tie,
Then snaps his visible braces
As he winks an invisible eye.

Last thing in his visible nightgown
Tucked up in his visible bed
He rests on a visible pillow
His weary invisible head

And ponders by visible moonlight
What invisibility means
Then drifts into silent invisible sleep
Full of wonderful visible dreams.

John Mole

Sky in the Pie!

Waiter, there's a sky in my pie
Remove it at once if you please
You can keep your incredible sunsets
I ordered mincemeat and cheese

I can't stand nightingales singing
Or clouds all burnished with gold
The whispering breeze is disturbing the peas
And making my chips go all cold

I don't care if the chef is an artist
Whose canvases hang in the Tate
I want two veg and puff pastry
Not the Universe heaped on my plate

OK I'll try just a spoonful
I suppose I've got nothing to lose
Mm . . . the colours quite tickle the palette
With a blend of delicate hues

The sun has a custardy flavour
And the clouds are as light as air
And the wind a chewier texture
(With a hint of cinnamon there?)

This sky is simply delicious
Why haven't I tried it before?
I can chew my way through to Eternity
And still have room left for more

Having acquired a taste for the Cosmos
I'll polish this sunset off soon
I can't wait to tuck into the night sky
Waiter! Please bring me the Moon!

Roger McGough

A Boat, Beneath a Sunny Sky

A boat, beneath a sunny sky,
Lingering onward dreamily
In an evening of July –

Children three that nestle near,
Eager eye and willing ear,
Pleased a simple tale to hear –

Long has paled that sunny sky:
Echoes fade and memories die:
Autumn frosts have slain July.

Still she haunts me, phantomwise,
Alice moving under skies
Never seen by waking eyes.

Children yet, the tale to hear,
Eager eye and willing ear,
Lovingly shall nestle near.

In a Wonderland they lie,
Dreaming as the days go by,
Dreaming as the summers die:

Ever drifting down the stream –
Lingering in the golden gleam –
Life, what is it but a dream?

Lewis Carroll

10

An Owl Flew in my Bedroom Once

My attic bedroom had two windows –
One that opened high above the street
And a skylight – a tile of thick glass
Like a see-through slate.
And through it fell the moonlight
Coring the darkness like an apple-peeler.
Suddenly in that long cylinder of light
Appeared the owl, mysterious and grey
In that cold moon.
He flew in silently – a piece of night adrift –
Escaped. He circled, didn't settle
On the banister or rail.
There was no rattle of his talons,
No gripe or stomp
To make him solid with their sound,
He simply floated in – turned wide – and floated out . . .
In the morning there was nothing
No down or limy dropping
Nothing to prove he'd ever been at all.

An owl flew in my bedroom once, I think.

Jan Dean

Bramble Talk

A caterpillar on a leaf
Said sadly to another:
'So many pretty butterflies . . .
I wonder which one's Mother.'

Richard Edwards

Swansong

Swan, swim over the sea.
 Swim, swan, swim!
Swan, swim back again.
 Well swum, swan.

Anon.

School in the Holidays

Down the corridors
nothing happens.

In the window's light
nobody moves.

The race is over,
the engine is cooling

and the school is like a driver
removing his gloves.

Ian McMillan

Ecclesiastes 3, 1–8

To every thing there is a season,
   and a time to every purpose under heaven:
A time to be born, and a time to die;
   a time to plant, and a time to pluck up that which is
      planted;
A time to kill, and a time to heal;
   a time to break down, and a time to build up;
A time to weep, and a time to laugh;
   a time to mourn, and a time to dance;
A time to cast away stones, and a time to gather stones
      together;
   a time to embrace, and a time to refrain from embracing;
A time to get, and a time to lose;
   a time to keep, and a time to cast away;
A time to rend, and a time to sew;
   a time to keep silence, and a time to speak;
A time to love, and a time to hate;
   a time of war, and a time of peace.

The Bible

Legend

The blacksmith's boy went out with a rifle
and a black dog running behind.
Cobwebs snatched at his feet,
rivers hindered him,
thorn-branches caught at his eyes to make him blind
and the sky turned into an unlucky opal,
but he didn't mind.
I can break branches, I can swim rivers, I can stare out any
    spider I meet,
said he to his dog and his rifle.

The blacksmith's boy went over the paddocks
with his old black hat on his head.
Mountains jumped in his way,
rocks rolled down on him,
and the old crow cried, You'll soon be dead;
and the rain came down like mattocks.
But he only said
I can climb mountains, I can dodge rocks, I can shoot an old
    crow any day.
And he went on over the paddocks.

When he came to the end of the day the sun began falling.
Up came the night ready to swallow him,
like the barrel of a gun,
like an old black hat,
like a black dog hungry to follow him.
Then the pigeon, the magpie and the dove began wailing,
and the grass lay down to pillow him.
His rifle broke, his hat blew away and his dog was gone,
and the sun was falling.

But in front of the night the rainbow stood on the mountain
just as his heart foretold.
He ran like a hare,
he climbed like a fox,
he caught it in his hands, the colours and the cold –
like a bar of ice, like the columns of a fountain,
like a ring of gold.
The pigeon, the magpie and the dove flew up to stare,
and the grass stood up again on the mountain.

The blacksmith's boy hung the rainbow on his shoulder,
instead of his broken gun.
Lizards ran out to see,
snakes made way for him,
and the rainbow shone as brightly as the sun.
All the world said, Nobody is braver, nobody is bolder,
nobody else has done
anything to equal it. He went home as easy as could be
with the swinging rainbow on his shoulder.

Judith Wright

Goldfish

the scene of the crime
was a goldfish bowl
goldfish were kept
in the bowl at the time:

that was the scene
and that was the crime

Alan Jackson

Topsy-Turvy World

If the butterfly courted the bee,
   And the owl the porcupine;
If churches were built in the sea,
   And three times one was nine;
If the pony rode his master,
   If the buttercups ate the cows,
If the cat had the dire disaster
   To be worried, sir, by the mouse;
If mamma, sir, sold the baby
   To a gypsy for half a crown;
If a gentleman, sir, was a lady,
   The world would be Upside-Down!
If any or all of these wonders
   Should ever come about,
I should not consider them blunders,
   For I should be Inside-Out!

William Brighty Rands

18

Into My Heart an Air that Kills

Into my heart an air that kills
   From yon far country blows:
What are those blue remembered hills,
   What spires, what farms are those?

That is the land of lost content,
   I see it shining plain,
The happy highways where I went
   And cannot come again.

A.E. Housman

Proverbial Logic

Where there are pandas
there's bamboo, but the converse
is sadly not true.

Debjani Chatterjee

Towards the End of Summer

Cherry red and honey bee
Buzzed around the Summer flowers
Bumbled round the luscious fruits.
Patient weaver clambered by.

Silently while the others bobbed
And busied in the bright blue air
Hither, zither, merrily,
Weaver waved his cool brown arms

And gently drew around the tree
Silken skeins so fine so fine
No one could see that they were there,
Until one Autumn morning when
Cherry was gone and bee asleep
A silver shawl was laced across the grass
With little beads like pearls strung all along.

Jenny Joseph

Lies

I like to go out for the day and tell lies.
The day should be overcast
with a kind of purple, electric edge to the clouds;
and not too hot or cold,
but cool. I turn up the collar of my coat
and narrow my eyes.

I meet someone –
a kid from school perhaps –
and give him five.
Then I start to lie
as we walk along Tennyson Drive kicking a can.
He listens hard,
his split strawberry mouth moist and mute;
my weasel words
sparking the little lights in his spectacles.
At the corner of Coleridge Place
I watch him run,
thrilled, fast, chasing his breath,
home to his mum.

Bus stops I like,
with long, bored, footsore, moaning queues.
I lie to them
in my shrill, confident voice,
till the number 8 or 11 takes them away
and I stand and stare at the bend in Longfellow Road,
alone in the day.

At the end of the darkening afternoon
I head for home,
watching the lights come on in truthful rooms,
where mothers come and go
with plates of cakes,
and TV sets shuffle their bright cartoons.
Then I knock on the door of 21 Wordsworth Way,
and while I wait
I watch a spaceship zoom away overhead
and see the faint half-smile of the distant moon.
They let me in.
And who, they want to know, do I think I am?
Exactly where have I been? With whom? And why?
The thing with me –
I like to come home after a long day out
and lie.

Carol Ann Duffy

The Grizzly Bear

The Grizzly Bear is huge and wild;
He has devoured the infant child.
The infant child is not aware
He has been eaten by the bear.

A.E. Housman

To *my Dear and Loving Husband*

If ever two were one, then surely we.
If ever man were loved by wife, then thee;
If ever wife was happy in a man,
Compare with me, ye women, if you can.
I prize thy love more than whole mines of gold
Or all the riches that the East doth hold.
My love is such that rivers cannot quench,
Nor ought but love from thee, give recompense.
Thy love is such I can no way repay,
The heavens reward thee manifold, I pray.
Then while we live, in love let's so persèvere
That when we live no more, we may live ever.

Anne Bradstreet

24

Jason's Trial

Jason was a football freak;
  He really loved the game:
To be a first-class footballer
  Was his one aim.

He practised every day and played
  Again each night in dream;
When he was twelve they chose him for
  The school's first team.

He was quite brilliant. Five years passed
  And – though rarely this occurs –
It seemed his dreams might all come true:
  He was given a trial by Spurs.

He played a blinder on the day;
  The spectators cheered and roared,
And after the match he was asked to appear
  Before the Selection Board.

The Chairman said, 'I've got the reports
   From our experts who watched you play:
Your speed and ball-control were fine;
   For tackling you get an A.

'And when our striker scored his goal
   You were first to jump on his back,
And when *you* scored you punched the air
   Before you resumed the attack.

'So far, so good; but you were weak
   On the thing our lads do best;
It seems you hardly spat at all,
   So you failed the spitting-test.

'But don't despair. If you go home
   And practise every day
You still might learn to spit with style
   In the true professional way.'

Vernon Scannell

For Forest

Forest could keep secrets
Forest could keep secrets

Forest tune in every day
to watersound and birdsound
Forest letting her hair down
to the teeming creeping of her forest-ground

But Forest don't broadcast her business
no Forest cover her business down
from sky and fast-eye sun
and when night come
and darkness wrap her like a gown
Forest is a bad dream woman

Forest dreaming about mountain
and when earth was young
Forest dreaming of the caress of gold
Forest rootsing with mysterious Eldorado

and when howler monkey
wake her up with howl
Forest just stretch and stir
to a new day of sound

but coming back to secrets
Forest could keep secrets
Forest could keep secrets

And we must keep Forest

Grace Nichols

In Praise of Noses

Not exactly ornamental
even when quite straight,
these funny, two-holed things!

But think:
if they faced upwards
they'd blow hats off

when one sneezed
and fill with rain
when it poured.

If sideways,
what objects of derision
snuff-takers would be!

Now all that a sneeze merits
is a 'God bless'.

God bless indeed, sweet nose,
warming, filtering,

humidifying the air as I breathe,
you do a marvellous job!

Prabhu S. Guptara

Epitaph for a Gifted Man

He was not known among his friends for wit;
He owned no wealth, nor did he crave for it.
His looks would never draw a second glance;
He could not play an instrument or dance,
Or sing, or paint, nor would he ever write
The music, plays, or poems that delight
And win the whole world's worship and applause.
He did not fight for any noble cause;
Showed neither great extravagance nor thrift;
But he loved greatly: that was his one gift.

Vernon Scannell

Under the Greenwood Tree

Under the greenwood tree,
Who loves to lie with me,
And turn his merry note
Unto the sweet bird's throat:
Come hither, come hither, come hither,
Here shall he see no enemy
But Winter and rough weather.

Who doth ambition shun,
And loves to live i' the Sun,
Seeking the food he eats,
And pleased with what he gets:
Come hither, come hither, come hither,
Here shall he see no enemy
But Winter and rough weather.

William Shakespeare

Something Told the Wild Geese

Something told the wild geese
    It was time to go.
Though the field lay golden
    Something whispered, 'Snow.'
Leaves were green and stirring,
    Berries, lustre-glossed,
But beneath warm feathers
    Something cautioned, 'Frost.'
All the sagging orchards
    Steamed with amber spice,
But each wild breast stiffened
    At remembered ice.
Something told the wild geese
    It was time to fly –
Summer sun was on their wings,
    Winter in their cry.

Rachel Field

In the Desert

Wrapped in my camelhair rug
I'm camouflaged
out here in the desert.
My feet make no sound on the sand.
The sky is crawling with stars.

I shout, and it echoes
all the way to the sea.
No answering cry comes back to me.
I could be the last boy,
I could be up on the moon.

Nothing but flat for miles,
the occasional bone
strewn on the sand.
I take one back with me
to help bury my parachute.

I check my compass
and head due south-east.
A light wind covers my footprints.
I have no need of water.
I'll hit the oasis by dawn.

Matthew Sweeney

Twenty Years Ago

Round the house were lilacs and strawberries
   And foal-foots spangling the paths,
And far away on the sand-hills, dewberries
   Caught dust from the sea's long swaths.

Up in the wolds the woods were walking,
   And nuts fell out of their hair.
At the gate the nets hung, balking
   The star-lit rush of a hare.

In the autumn fields, the stubble
   Tinkled in music of gleaning.
At a mother's knee, the trouble
   Lost all its meaning.

Yea, what good beginnings
   To this sad end!
Have we had our innings?
   God forfend!

D.H. Lawrence

September

The Day that Summer Died

From all around the mourners came
　The day that Summer died,
From hill and valley, field and wood
　And lake and mountainside.

They did not come in funeral black
　But every mourner chose
Gorgeous colours or soft shades
　Of russet, yellow, rose.

Horse chestnut, oak and sycamore
　Wore robes of gold and red;
The rowan sported scarlet beads;
　No bitter tears were shed;

Although at dusk the mourners heard,
   As a small wind softly sighed,
A touch of sadness in the air
   The day that Summer died.

Vernon Scannell

Poppies

Cold reigns the summer, and grey falls the day,
The flame of the year is smouldering away,
But here in the hedgerow and yonder in the wheat
The flame of the poppy is throwing out its heat.

Small grows the corn and scant is the yield
Of the hay lying strewn upon the stubble field,
And there in the meadow and here by the road
The red poppy glows as in other years it glowed.

Sunrise comes chilly and sunset comes wet,
And low burns the flame where the sun rose and set,
But red as the flame of a dawn that will not pass
The fire of the poppy is lighted in the grass.

Eleanor Farjeon

Abou Ben Adhem

Abou Ben Adhem (may his tribe increase!)
Awoke one night from a deep dream of peace,
And saw, within the moonlight in his room,
Making it rich, and like a lily in bloom,
An Angel writing in a book of gold:

Exceeding peace had made Ben Adhem bold,
And to the Presence in the room he said,
'What writest thou?' The Vision raised its head,
And with a look made of all sweet accord
Answered, 'The names of those who love the Lord.'

'And is mine one?' said Abou. 'Nay, not so,'
Replied the Angel. Abou spoke more low,
But cheerly still; and said, 'I pray thee, then,
Write me as one that loves his fellow-men.'

The Angel wrote, and vanished. The next night
It came again with a great wakening light,
And showed the names whom love of God had blessed,
And, lo! Ben Adhem's name led all the rest!

Leigh Hunt

One, Two, Three, Four, Five

One, two, three, four, five,
Once I caught a fish alive,
Six, seven, eight, nine, ten,
Then I let it go again.
Why did you let it go?
Because it bit my finger so.
Which finger did it bite?
This little finger on the right.

Anon.

Bird

Something fluttered about my heart
Like a bird caught in a snare
I blame the girl on the fourteen bus
It was she who put it there.

Gareth Owen

Mr Baggs

I was walking home from school
with Mr Baggs
the teacher who took us for football
and he said:
'You see, Michael, what we need in the team
is a really good centre-half,
someone who can control the game from midfield
collect the ball in the middle
distribute the ball to the front players.
A good centre-half can turn a game.
He can make all the difference.
Now who have we got playing in the middle?
– oh, my goodness it's you
I forgot
I'm sorry
I wasn't thinking
no hard feelings, OK?'

Michael Rosen

Whisky Frisky

Whisky frisky.
Hipperty hop,
Up he goes
To the tree top!

Whirly, twirly,
Round and round,
Down he scampers
To the ground.

Furly, curly,
What a tail,
Tall as a feather,
Broad as a sail.

Where's his supper?
In the shell.
Snappy, cracky,
Out it fell.

Anon.

For the Fallen
(September 1914)

With proud thanksgiving, a mother for her children,
England mourns for her dead across the sea.
Flesh of her flesh they were, spirit of her spirit,
Fallen in the cause of the free.

Solemn the drums thrill: Death august and royal
Sings sorrow up into immortal spheres.
There is music in the midst of desolation
And a glory that shines upon our tears.

They went with songs to the battle, they were young,
Straight of limb, true of eye, steady and aglow.
They were staunch to the end against odds uncounted,
They fell with their faces to the foe.

They shall grow not old, as we that are left grow old:
Age shall not weary them, nor the years condemn.
At the going down of the sun and in the morning
We will remember them.

They mingle not with their laughing comrades again;
They sit no more at familiar tables of home;
They have no lot in our labour of the day-time;
They sleep beyond England's foam.

But where our desires are and our hopes profound,
Felt as a well-spring that is hidden from sight,
To the innermost heart of their own land they are known
As the stars are known to the Night;

As the stars that shall be bright when we are dust,
Moving in marches upon the heavenly plain,
As the stars that are starry in the time of our darkness,
To the end, to the end, they remain.

Laurence Binyon

Cat Warmth

All afternoon,
My cat sleeps,
On the end of my bed.

When I creep my toes
Down between the cold sheets,
I find a patch of cat-warmth
That he's left behind;
An invisible gift.

John Cunliffe

She Dwelt Among the Untrodden Ways

She dwelt among the untrodden ways
    Beside the springs of Dove,
A Maid whom there were none to praise
    And very few to love:

A violet by a mossy stone
    Half-hidden from the eye!
– Fair as a star, when only one
    Is shining in the sky.

She lived unknown, and few could know
    When Lucy ceased to be;
But she is in her grave, and, oh,
    The difference to me!

William Wordsworth

The Tomcat of Notre Dame

High above the roofs of Paris
Lives the Tomcat of Notre Dame
Looking down at the passers-by
Ready to save them from harm

The River Seine below him
He watches the boats go by
All set to swing to the rescue
In a twinkling of an eye

Catching a baby pigeon
Or a puppy from under a bus
Saving a drowning kitten
Never making a fuss

The bells have made him slightly deaf
But he'll never miss a call
Swinging down a bell-rope
Clambering down a wall

Amid the wheels and pulleys
And the thunderous sound of bells
Lonely amongst the gargoyles
He'll sometimes pull faces as well

The lovely Esmerelda
Is the apple of his eye
Green-eyed, black and slinky
He sees her with a sigh

'She's the Belle of the Flower Market
The toast of Gay Paree
All the young toms serenade her
How *could* she love someone like me?

She should have a cosy home
With cream and a welcome mat
Not a corner of a tower alone
With a poor Cathedral cat'

And then one summer evening
Perched on top of a spire
Listening to the organ
And the singing of the choir

He heard a sound from far below
A muffled miaow for help
He sprang from peak to pinnacle
Not caring if he fell

September

From a darkened doorway
There came a scuffling sound
Two rough cats were struggling
With a figure on the ground

Downwards on a rope he swung
Sending the villains flying
Through the dusk he swarmed back up
His trembling burden crying

Behind a flying buttress
He laid it on the floor
Two green eyes slowly opened
She gently took his paw

'My hero! If you want me
I'll stay and share your life
Up here above the rooftops
I'll be your loving wife'

Now they're together paw-in-paw
She'll never come to harm
The lovely Esmerelda
And the Tomcat of Notre Dame

High above the roofs of Paris
Live the Tomcat and his Madame
As the sun sets over the River Seine
And the towers of Notre Dame.

Adrian Henri

No Points

September, and my team
has got no points;
played six, lost six.

Our season
has creaking joints;
played six, won none.

September, and my team
are rolling down a hill
called Played Six, Lost Six.

Our season
is feeling ill
with Played Six, Won None.

Ian and Andrew McMillan

As the Team's Head-Brass

As the team's head-brass flashed out on the turn
The lovers disappeared into the wood.
I sat among the boughs of the fallen elm
That strewed the angle of the fallow, and
Watched the plough narrowing a yellow square
Of charlock. Every time the horses turned
Instead of treading me down, the ploughman leaned
Upon the handles to say or ask a word,
About the weather, next about the war.
Scraping the share he faced towards the wood,
And screwed along the furrow till the brass flashed
Once more.
                    The blizzard felled the elm whose crest
I sat in, by a woodpecker's round hole,
The ploughman said. 'When will they take it away?'
'When the war's over.' So the talk began
One minute and an interval of ten,
A minute more and the same interval.

'Have you been out?' 'No.' 'And don't want to, perhaps?'
'If I could only come back again, I should.
I could spare an arm. I shouldn't want to lose
A leg. If I should lose my head, why, so,
I should want nothing more . . . Have many gone
From here?' 'Yes.' 'Many lost?' 'Yes, a good few.
Only two teams work on the farm this year.
One of my mates is dead. The second day
In France they killed him. It was back in March,
The very night of the blizzard, too. Now if
He had stayed here we should have moved the tree.'
'And I should not have sat here. Everything
Would have been different. For it would have been
Another world.' 'Ay, and a better, though
If we could see all all might seem good.' Then
The lovers came out of the wood again:
The horses started and for the last time
I watched the clods crumble and topple over
After the ploughshare and the stumbling team.

Edward Thomas

Water Everywhere

There's water on the ceiling,
And water on the wall,
There's water in the bedroom,
And water in the hall,
There's water on the landing,
And water on the stair,
Whenever Daddy takes a bath
There's water everywhere.

Valerie Bloom

Symphony in Yellow

An omnibus across the bridge
   Crawls like a yellow butterfly,
   And, here and there, a passer-by
Shows like a little restless midge.

Big barges full of yellow hay
   Are moored against the shadowy wharf,
   And, like a yellow silken scarf,
The thick fog hangs along the quay.

The yellow leaves begin to fade
   And flutter from the Temple elms,
   And at my feet the pale green Thames
Lies like a rod of rippled jade.

Oscar Wilde

Grandpa's Soup

No one makes soup like my Grandpa's,
with its diced carrots the perfect size
and its diced potatoes the perfect size
and its wee soft bits –
what are their names?
and its big bit of hough,
which rhymes with loch, floating
like a rich island in the middle of the soup sea.

I say, Grandpa, Grandpa, your soup is the best soup in the
    whole world.
And Grandpa says, Och,
which rhymes with hough and loch.
Och, don't be daft,
because he's shy about his soup, my Grandpa.
He knows I will grow up and pine for it.
I will get ill and desperately need it.
I will long for it my whole life after he is gone.
Every soup will become sad and wrong after he is gone.

He knows when I'm older I will avoid soup altogether.
Oh Grandpa, Grandpa, why is your soup so glorious? I say
tucking into my fourth bowl in a day.

Barley! That's the name of the wee soft bits. Barley.

Jackie Kay

Growler

Like a toad
beneath a suddenly
flipped stone

huffed up
as if about
to sing (but no

sound comes)
yes, it was me.
I was the one

who cracked the bell
of everyone's *Hey-*
Ring-A-Ding-Ding-

Sweet-Lovers-Love-the . . .
'Stop!' Miss Carver
clapped her hands.

'Which one of you's
the Growler?' No one
breathed. 'Very well.

Sing on.' And she leaned
very close
all down the line till

'Stop!'
She was as small as me
(aged eight)

but sour and sixty,
savage for the love
of her sweet music

I was curdling.
'You!
How *dare* you?

Out!' Down the echoing
hall, all eyes on me . . .
My one big solo.

She died last year.
I hope somebody sang.
Me, I'm still growling.

Philip Gross

Woolly Mammoth

He grazed sweet upland pasture,
crushing spring flowers
with hairy elephant feet,
methodically eating.
But sweeter plants grew
at the torrent fringe;
his long tusks clunked the stones,
trying the edge,

too far.

His roar shook snow
to plunge with him
into the crevasse where he lay,
ice-cradled, for centuries.

Discovered by explorers
after fifty thousand years
he was still wrapped in chestnut hair;
the broken tusks
were fossil ivory.
In his mouth were remnants of
the last surprising meal;
buttercups and orchids.

Irene Rawnsley

The Tiger

The Tiger, on the other hand, is kittenish and mild,
He makes a pretty playfellow for any little child;
And mothers of large families (who claim to common sense)
Will find a Tiger well repay the trouble and expense.

Hilaire Belloc

Saturdays

Real
Genuine
Saturdays
Like marbles
Conkers
Sweet new potatoes
Have their especial season
Are all morning
With midday at five o'clock.
True Saturdays
Are borrowed from early Winter
And the left overs
Of Autumn sunshine days
But separate from days of snow.
The skies dine on dwindles of smoke
Where leafy plots smoulder
With small fires.
Sunday meat is bought
And late
Large, white loaves
From little corner shops.

September

People passing
Wave over garden walls,
Greengrocers and milkmen are smiled upon
And duly paid.
It is time for the chequered tablecloth
And bowls of soup.
And early on
We set out with some purpose
Through only
Lovely Saturday,
Under skies
Like sun-shot water,
For the leccy train
And the Match in Liverpool.

Gareth Owen

Prior Knowledge

Prior Knowledge was a strange boy.
He had sad green eyes.
He always seemed to know when I was telling lies.

We were friends for a summer.
Prior got out his knife
and mixed our bloods so we'd be brothers for life.

You'll be rich, he said, and famous;
but I must die.
Then brave, clever Prior began to cry.

He knew so much.
He knew the day before
I'd drop a jam jar full of frogspawn on the kitchen floor.

He knew there were wasps
in the gardening gloves.
He knew the name of the girl I'd grow up to love.

The day he died
he knew there would be
a wind shaking conkers from the horse chestnut tree;

and an aimless child
singing down Prior's street,
with bright red sandals on her skipping feet.

Carol Ann Duffy

Chook, Chook, Chook

Chook, chook, chook, chook, chook,
  Good morning, Mrs Hen.
How many chickens have you got?
  Madam, I've got ten.
Four of them are yellow,
  And four of them are brown,
And two of them are speckled red,
  The nicest in the town.

Anon.

The Inchcape Rock

No stir in the air, no stir in the sea;
The ship was still as she could be;
Her sails from heaven received no motion;
Her keel was steady in the ocean.

Without either sign or sound of their shock,
The waves flowed over the Inchcape Rock;
So little they rose, so little they fell,
They did not move the Inchcape Bell.

The worthy Abbot of Aberbrothok
Had placed that bell on the Inchcape Rock;
On a buoy in the storm it floated and swung,
And over the waves its warning rung.

When the rock was hid by the surge's swell,
The mariners heard the warning bell;
And then they knew the perilous rock,
And blest the Abbot of Aberbrothok.

The sun in heaven was shining gay,
All things were joyful on that day;
The sea birds screamed as they wheeled around,
And there was joyance in their sound.

The buoy of the Inchcape Bell was seen,
A darker speck on the ocean green.
Sir Ralph the Rover walked his deck,
And he fixed his eye on the darker speck.

He felt the cheering power of Spring;
It made him whistle; it made him sing;
His heart was mirthful to excess;
But the Rover's mirth was wickedness.

His eye was on the Inchcape float;
Quoth he, 'My men, put out the boat,
And row me to the Inchcape Rock,
And I'll plague the Abbot of Aberbrothok.'

The boat is lowered; the boatmen row,
And so to the Inchcape Rock they go.
Sir Ralph bent over from the boat,
And he cut the bell from the Inchcape float.

Down sank the bell with a gurgling sound,
The bubbles rose and burst around.
Quoth Sir Ralph, 'The next who comes to the Rock
Won't bless the Abbot of Aberbrothok.'

Sir Ralph the Rover sailed away;
He scoured the seas for many a day,
And now, grown rich with plundered store,
He steers his course for Scotland's shore.

So thick a haze o'erspreads the sky
They cannot see the sun on high,
The wind hath blown a gale all day;
At evening it hath died away.

On deck the Rover takes his stand;
So dark it is they see no land.
Quoth Sir Ralph, 'It will be lighter soon,
For there is the dawn of the rising moon.'

'Canst hear,' said one, 'the breaker's roar?
For methinks we should be near the shore.'
'Now where we are I cannot tell;
But I wish I could hear the Inchcape Bell!'

They hear no sound; the swell is strong;
Though the wind hath fallen they drift along,
Till the vessel strikes with a shivering shock –
'Oh heavens! it is the Inchcape Rock!'

Sir Ralph the Rover tore his hair;
He cursed himself in his despair.
The waves rush in on every side;
The ship is sinking beneath the tide.

But even now, in his dying fear
One dreadful sound could the Rover hear –
A sound as if, with the Inchcape Bell,
The fiends in triumph were ringing his knell.

Robert Southey

Will it go to a Replay?

Last night's cup-tie
Everton and Sheffield United
was so exciting, really tough.

Two teams battled it out
through the rain and mud
as goal after goal
thudded into the net.

The crowd went wild
just loved
every nail-biting moment.

Four-four
with five minutes left
of extra time
both teams down to nine men
and the tension tightening.

In those dying minutes
both sides
cleared their goal lines
with desperate headers.

Everton missed a penalty
United missed an open goal.

With seconds to go
a replay at Bramall Lane
seemed certain, until

Everton had to go in for her tea
and Sheffield United went to the shops
for his mum.

David Harmer

The Apple Raid

Darkness came early, though not yet cold;
Stars were strung on the telegraph wires;
Street lamps spilled pools of liquid gold;
The breeze was spiced with garden fires.

That smell of burnt leaves, the early dark,
Can still excite me but not as it did
So long ago when we met in the Park –
Myself, John Peters and David Kidd.

We moved out of town to the district where
The lucky and wealthy had their homes
With garages, gardens, and apples to spare
Ripely clustered in the trees' green domes.

We chose the place we meant to plunder
And climbed the wall and dropped down to
The secret dark. Apples crunched under
Our feet as we moved through the grass and dew.

September

The clusters on the lower boughs of the tree
Were easy to reach. We stored the fruit
In pockets and jerseys until all three
Boys were heavy with their tasty loot.

Safe on the other side of the wall
We moved back to town and munched as we went.
I wonder if David remembers at all
That little adventure, the apples' fresh scent?

Strange to think that he's fifty years old,
That tough little boy with scabs on his knees;
Stranger to think that John Peters lies cold
In an orchard in France beneath apple trees.

Vernon Scannell

Myfanwy Among the Leaves

Dying leaf and dead leaf,
Yellow leaf and red leaf
And white-backed beam,
Lay long the woodland road
As quiet as a dream.

Summer was over,
The year had lost her lover,
Spent with a grief
All along the woodland road
Leaf fell on leaf.

Then came a shuffling,
Such a happy ruffling
Of the dried sweet
Surf of leaves upon the road
Round a baby's feet.

Year-old leaf ran after
Three-year-old laughter,
Danced through the air
As she caught them from the road
And flung them anywhere.

Old leaf and cold leaf,
Brown leaf and gold leaf
And white-backed beam,
Followed down the woodland road
Myfanwy in a dream.

Eleanor Farjeon

My Father

Some fathers work at the office, others work at the store,
Some operate great cranes and build up skyscrapers galore,
Some work in canning factories counting green peas into
  cans,
Some drive all night in huge and thundering removal vans.

But mine has the strangest job of the lot.
My Father's the Chief Inspector of – What?
O don't tell the mice, don't tell the moles,
My Father's the Chief Inspector of H O L E S.

It's a work of the highest importance because you never know
What's in a hole, what fearful thing is creeping from below.
Perhaps it's a hole to the ocean and will soon gush water in tons,
Or maybe it leads to a vast cave full of gold and skeletons.

Though a hole might seem to have nothing but dirt in,
Somebody's simply got to make certain.
Caves in the mountain, clefts in the wall,
My Father has to inspect them all.

That crack in the road looks harmless. My Father knows it's not.
The world may be breaking into two and starting at that spot.
Or maybe the world is a great egg, and we live on the shell,
And it's just beginning to split and hatch: you simply cannot tell.

If you see a crack, run to the phone, run!
My Father will know just what's to be done.
A rumbling hole, a silent hole,
My Father will soon have it under control.

Keeping a check on all these holes he hurries from morning
   to night.
There might be sounds of marching in one, or an eye shining
   bright.
A tentacle came groping from a hole that belonged to a
   mouse,
A floor collapsed and Chinamen swarmed up into the house.

A Hole's an unpredictable thing –
Nobody knows what a Hole might bring.
Caves in the mountain, clefts in the wall,
My Father has to inspect them all!

Ted Hughes

Summer Romance

I was best friends with Sabah
the whole long summer;
I admired her handwriting,
the way she smiled into
the summer evening,
her voice, melted butter.
The way her chin shone
under a buttercup.
Everyone let Sabah
go first in a long
hot summer queue.
The way she always looked
fancy, the way
she said 'Fandango',
and plucked her banjo;
her big purple bangle
banged at her wrist;
her face lit by the angle
poise lamp in her room,
her hair all a tangle,
damp from the summer heat,
Sabah's eyes sparkled all summer.

But when the summer was gone
and the winter came,
in walked Big Heather Murphy.
Sabah turned her lovely head
towards her. I nearly died.
Summer holidays burn with lies.

Jackie Kay

Digging

Today I think
Only with scents, – scents dead leaves yield,
And bracken, and wild carrot's seed,
And the square mustard field;

Odours that rise
When the spade wounds the root of tree,
Rose, currant, raspberry, or goutweed,
Rhubarb or celery;

The smoke's smell, too,
Flowing from where a bonfire burns
The dead, the waste, the dangerous,
And all to sweetness turns.

It is enough
To smell, to crumble the dark earth,
While the robin sings over again
Sad songs of Autumn mirth.

Edward Thomas

Greengrocer

I went into the greengrocer's:
the vegetables and the fruit
were all piled neatly in their boxes
and a large watermelon lay in the corner.

I couldn't see the greengrocer.
The shop smelt ripe and drowsy. I put
three bananas in a paper bag. It was
so still and silent I felt watched.
The mushrooms looked like knee bones.
The watermelon lay contented in the corner.

What had happened to the greengrocer?
I took some carrots. I stuffed
plastic bags with spinach,
with the long green teeth of okra,
with courgettes like tiny truncheons.
The watermelons lay big-bellied in the corner.

There was no sign of the greengrocer.
I called out, I waited, then I left
money by the till and went towards the door.
The enormous watermelon in the corner
snored.

Dave Calder

October

Dance to your Daddy

Dance to your daddy,
My little babby,
Dance to your daddy,
My little lamb;

You shall have a fishy
In a little dishy,
You shall have a fishy
When the boat comes in.

Anon.

Windy Nights

Whenever the moon and stars are set,
   Whenever the wind is high,
All night long in the dark and wet,
   A man goes riding by.
Late in the night when the fires are out,
Why does he gallop and gallop about?

Whenever the trees are crying aloud,
   And ships are tossed at sea,
By, on the highway, low and loud,
   By at the gallop goes he.
By at the gallop he goes, and then
By he comes back at the gallop again.

Robert Louis Stevenson

The Wild Yorkshire Pudding

On moors we are hunting
The wild Yorkshire pudding;
The small ones are nippy,
The fat ones are grunting.

They snuggle together
And hide in the heather;
The young ones are tasty,
The old ones like leather.

We jump on and snatch 'em;
They shriek as we catch 'em;
On cords which take twenty
We string and attach 'em.

They dry them in Batley;
They can them in Ilkley.
You will find they are served
Where menus are stately.

Our terriers are scenting
The rock-crevice-skulking
Tremendous with gravy
And wild Yorkshire pudding.

Alan Dixon

Throwing a Tree
New Forest

The two executioners stalk along over the knolls,
Bearing two axes with heavy heads shining and wide,
And a long limp two-handled saw toothed for cutting
    great boles,
And so they approach the proud tree that bears the death-
    mark on its side.

October

Jackets doffed they swing axes and chop away just above
   ground,
And the chips fly about and lie white on the moss and
   fallen leaves;
Till a broad deep gash in the bark is hewn all the way
   round,
And one of them tries to hook upward a rope, which at least
   he achieves.

The saw then begins, till the top of the tall giant shivers:
The shivers are seen to grow greater each cut than before:
They edge out the saw, tug the rope; but the tree only
   quivers,
And kneeling and sawing again, they step back to try pulling
   once more.

Then lastly, the living mast sways, further sways: with a
   shout
Job and Ike rush aside. Reached the end of its long
   staying powers
The tree crashes downward: it shakes all its neighbours
   throughout,
And two hundred years' steady growth has been ended in
   less than two hours.

Thomas Hardy

5

St Jerome and his Lion

St Jerome in his study kept a great big cat,
It's always in his pictures, with its feet upon the mat.
Did he give it milk to drink, in a little dish?
When it came to Fridays, did he give it fish?
If I lost my little cat, I'd be sad without it;
I should ask St Jeremy what to do about it;
I should ask St Jeremy, just because of that,
For he's the only saint I know who kept a pussy cat.

Anon.

Conkers

Autumn treasures
from the horsechestnut tree

Lying roly poly
among their split green casings

Shiny and hard
like pops of polished mahogany

An English schoolboy
picking them up –

The same compulsive
fickle avidity –

As I picked up
orange-coloured cockles

Way back then
from a tropical childhood tree

October

Hand about to close in . . .
then spotting another even better

Now, waiting on our bus
we grown-ups watch him

Not knowing how or why
we've lost our instinct

For gathering
the magic shed of trees

Though in partyful mood
in wineful spirits

We dance around crying,
'Give me back my conker.'

Grace Nichols

The Charge of the Light Brigade

Half a league, half a league,
Half a league onward,
All in the valley of Death
　Rode the six hundred.
　'Forward, the Light Brigade!
Charge for the guns!' he said.
Into the valley of Death
　Rode the six hundred.

'Forward, the Light Brigade!'
Was there a man dismayed?
Not though the soldier knew
　Some one had blundered.
Theirs not to make reply,
Theirs not to reason why,
Theirs but to do and die.
Into the valley of Death
　Rode the six hundred.

Cannon to right of them,
Cannon to left of them,
Cannon in front of them
   Volleyed and thundered;
Stormed at with shot and shell,
Boldly they rode and well,
Into the jaws of Death,
Into the mouth of Hell
   Rode the six hundred.

Flashed all the sabres bare,
Flashed as they turned in air
Sabring the gunners there,
Charging an army, while
   All the world wondered:
Plunged in the battery-smoke
Right through the line they broke;
Cossack and Russian
Reeled from the sabre-stroke
   Shattered and sundered.
Then they rode back, but not,
   Not the six hundred.

Cannon to right of them,
Cannon to left of them,
Cannon behind them
  Volleyed and thundered;
Stormed at with shot and shell,
While horse and hero fell,
They that had fought so well
Came through the jaws of Death,
Back from the mouth of Hell,
All that was left of them,
  Left of six hundred.

When can their glory fade?
O the wild charge they made!
  All the world wondered.
Honour the charge they made!
Honour the Light Brigade,
  Noble six hundred!

Alfred Lord Tennyson

It's not the same anymore

It's not the same since Patch died.
Sticks are just sticks.
Never thrown, never fetched.

It's not the same anymore.
Tennis balls lie still and lifeless.
The urge to bounce them has gone.

It's not the same now.
I can't bring myself to whistle.
There's no reason to do so.

His collar hangs on the hook
and his name tag and lead are dusty.

His basket and bowl are in a plastic bag
lying at an angle on a garage shelf.

My new slippers will never be chewed
and I've no excuse for my lack of homework anymore.

I can now watch the football in peace, uninterrupted.
No frantic barking and leaping just when it gets to the goal.

I don't have to share my sweets and biscuits
and then wipe the dribbling drool off my trouser legs.

It's just not the same anymore.
When Patch died a small part of me died too.

All that's left is a mound of earth
and my hand made cross beneath the apple tree.

All that's left are the memories.
Thousands of them.

It's just not the same anymore.

Paul Cookson

The Tunneller

At number 42
there's a hawthorn perimeter hedge
and the front gate is topped
with strands of barbed wire.
The mad Major lives there,
a septuagenarian ex-soldier
with military moustache
and a broom-handle-straight back.

On a mission,
in the last War, he parachuted into Germany,
was captured, and then held
in a prison camp: Stalag number 39.
He tunnelled out, escaped to England.
His true story is printed in a book
I found at the library:
Spies of the Second World War.

Yesterday
at dusk, I hid in his long back garden
and spied on the Major
as he passed the old air-raid shelter
and marched into his garden shed.
He was dressed in black –
trousers, sweater, and woolly Balaclava.
Dirt streaks disguised his face.

I sneaked up
and through the cobwebby window
watched as the Major removed floorboards,
then lowered himself into a hole
and . . . disappeared!
He was tunnelling again,
digging beneath his back garden,
tunnelling towards the perimeter hedge.

An hour later
he emerged furtively from the shed
lugging a heavy sack
and I saw him scatter damp soil
between his rhubarb and cauliflowers.
Night after night he's at it,
secretly tunnelling his way to freedom,
trying to escape from Stalag number 42.

Wes Magee

Ghost Hunt

Long after midnight (whoo-whoo)
I searched for the haunted house (whoo-whoo),
but I didn't see
   a speck of a spectre
   a fraction of a phantom
   a spot of a spook
   a pinch of a poltergeist.
I didn't even catch the sweet scent
of a skellington's wellingtons!

Long after midnight (whoo-whoo)
I searched for the haunted house (whoo-whoo)
but when I couldn't find it
– well, I just gave up the ghost.

John Rice

11

from *The Highwayman*

The wind was a torrent of darkness among the gusty trees,
The moon was a ghostly galleon tossed upon cloudy seas,
The road was a ribbon of moonlight over the purple moor,
And the highwayman came riding –
    Riding – riding –
The highwayman came riding, up to the old inn-door.

He'd a French cocked-hat on his forehead, a bunch of lace
   at his chin,
A coat of claret velvet, and breeches of brown doe-skin;
They fitted with never a wrinkle: his boots were up to the
   thigh!
And he rode with a jewelled tinkle,
    His pistol butts a-twinkle,
His rapier hilt a-twinkle, under the jewelled sky.

Over the cobbles he clattered and clashed in the dark inn-
yard,
And he tapped with his whip on the shutters, but all was
locked and barred;
He whistled a tune to the window, and who should be
waiting there
But the landlord's black-eyed daughter,
Bess, the landlord's daughter,
Plaiting a dark red love-knot into her long black hair.

And dark in the old inn-yard a stable-wicket creaked
Where Tim the ostler listened; his face was white and
peaked;
His eyes were hollows of madness, his hair like mouldy hay,
But he loved the landlord's daughter,
The landlord's red-lipped daughter;
Dumb as a dog he listened, and he heard the robber say –

'One kiss, my bonny sweetheart, I'm after a prize tonight,
But I shall be back with the yellow gold before the morning
light;
Yet, if they press me sharply, and harry me through the day,
Then look for me by moonlight,
Watch for me by moonlight,
I'll come to thee by moonlight, though hell should bar the
way.'

He rose upright in the stirrups; he scarce could reach her
  hand,
But she loosened her hair i' the casement! His face burnt like
  a brand
As the black cascade of perfume came tumbling over his
  breast;
And he kissed its waves in the moonlight,
     (Oh, sweet black waves in the moonlight!)
Then he tugged at his rein in the moonlight, and galloped
  away to the west.

Alfred Noyes

Potty

Don't put that potty on your head, Tim.
Don't put that potty on your head.
  It's not very clean
  And you don't know where it's been,
So don't put that potty on your head.

Colin McNaughton

Fall, Leaves, Fall

Fall, leaves, fall; die, flowers, away;
Lengthen night and shorten day;
Every leaf speaks bliss to me
Fluttering from the autumn tree.

I shall smile when wreaths of snow
Blossom where the rose should grow;
I shall sing when night's decay
Ushers in a drearier day.

Emily Brontë

Bedtime

The night comes down on foxes
As they run across the hill,
The night comes down on fallow deer
That wander where they will,

The night comes down on white owls
As they wake in hollow trees,
The night comes down on badgers, free
To snuffle where they please,

The night comes down like velvet
On this house, and tenderly,
With starry streams and endless dreams
The night comes down on me.

Richard Edwards

Out of Season

It's October, and the sun
won't hang about too long
in this broken neck of the woods.

The coaches have stopped arriving.
July, August have sizzled briefly
like chips thrown into the pan

    and in the breeze
    the trees
    are hands
    shaking with age.

All over the country
in grey village squares like this
under sky
the colour of an old man's cardigan
the year shuffles into winter,

and the village's six children
if they lived near the sea
would walk by the sea.

October

Instead they walk
from the phone box
to the bus stop

and from the phone box
to the fish and chip caravan.

This is a postcard
no one sends home. Nobody
wishes they were here.

From the phone box
you can see the bus stop
and little else

and in the breeze
the trees
are hands
shaking with age.

Ian McMillan

Hide and Seek

Hide and seek, says the Wind,
  In the shade of the woods;
Hide and seek, says the Moon,
  To the hazel buds;
Hide and seek, says the Cloud,
  Star on to star;
Hide and seek, says the Wave
  At the harbour bar;
Hide and seek, says I,
  To myself, and step
Out of the dream of Wake
  Into the dream of Sleep.

Walter de la Mare

Wonder

Collie puppies in a dooryard,
Wheeling along lopsided,
So hard to manage those hind legs,
Standing, blue eyes on nothing,
Noses twitching,
Stubby tails in the air,
Trying to remember what they are thinking about:

Fat puppies that forget everything,
Even the terrible
White teeth their mother yaps at them
When she eats her supper:

Fat puppies full of wonder
At round holes where spiders live,
At the wide wings of a yellow butterfly,
And lifting shrill voices of wonder
At the stranger who leans over their gate
Making uncouth noises.

Bernard Raymund

Fear No More the Heat o' the Sun

Fear no more the heat o' the sun,
　Nor the furious winter's rages;
Thou thy worldly task hast done,
　Home art gone, and ta'en thy wages.
Golden lads and girls all must,
As chimney-sweepers, come to dust.

Fear no more the frown o' the great,
　Thou art past the tyrant's stroke;
Care no more to clothe and eat,
　To thee the reed is as the oak.
The sceptre, learning, physic, must
All follow this, and come to dust.

Fear no more the lightning-flash,
　Nor the all-dreaded thunder-stone;
Fear not slander, censure rash;
　Thou hast finished joy and moan.
All lovers young, all lovers must
Consign to thee, and come to dust.

William Shakespeare

Getting Back Home

Hang your hat on the peg
Rest up, rest up
Fling your coat on the bed
For you have travelled many miles to see me.

Put your feet on the bench
Rest up, rest up
Heave off your heavy boots
For you have come through Winter days to see me.

Settle down by the fire
Rest up, rest up
Lean back and smile at me
For after all this time and travelling
Oh traveller, I'm glad to see you.

Jenny Joseph

Four Crazy Pets

I've four crazy pets, all rather jolly –
Rover, Tiddles, Flopsy and Polly.
A dog, a rabbit, a parrot and a cat.
Which one's which? Can you guess that?

Rover's a dog? No!
Tiddles is a cat? No!
Flopsy's a rabbit? No!
Polly's a parrot? No!

My dog has the appetite of a small gorilla.
We called her Polly 'cause we can never fill her.

The rabbit has a habit of wetting where we're standing.
We call him Tiddles 'cause the puddles keep expanding.

Our cat purrs like an engine turning over
Vroom vroom vroom – so we call her Rover.

The fact that our parrot cannot fly is such a shame.
Flopsy by nature and Flopsy by name.

Four crazy names! Wouldn't you agree?
I think my pets fit their names purrfectly.

Paul Cookson

When I was One-and-Twenty

When I was one-and-twenty
  I heard a wise man say,
'Give crowns and pounds and guineas
  But not your heart away;
Give pearls away and rubies
  But keep your fancy free.'
But I was one-and-twenty,
  No use to talk to me.

When I was one-and-twenty
  I heard him say again,
'The heart out of the bosom
  Was never given in vain;
'Tis paid with sighs a plenty
  And sold for endless rue.'
And I am two-and-twenty,
  And oh, 'tis true, 'tis true.

A.E. Housman

Late Autumn

The boy called to his team
  And with blue-glancing share
Turned up the rape and turnip
  With yellow charlock to spare.

The long lean thistles stood
  Like beggars ragged and blind,
Half their white silken locks
  Blown away on the wind.

But I thought not once of winter
  Or summer that was past
Till I saw that slant-legged robin
  With autumn on his chest.

Andrew Young

Driving Home

Coming back home from Granny's in the car
I try to stay awake. I really do.
I look around to find the evening star
And make a wish. Who knows? It might come true.

I watch the yellow windows whizzing by
And sometimes see a person in a room,
Cutting a loaf of bread, tying a tie,
Stretching, or watching telly in the gloom.

I see the street lamps flash past, one by one,
And watch how people's shadows grow and shrink.
It's like a trick; I wonder how it's done.
I breathe and watch, and settle back to think.

But everything gets mixed and far away;
I feel I'm moving but I don't know where.
I hear a distant voice which seems to say,
'Wake up! (She's fast asleep.) Wake up! We're there!'

Gerard Benson

Ready Salted

Nothing else happened
That day.

Nothing much, anyway.

I got up, went to school,
Did the usual stuff.

Came home, watched telly,
Did the usual stuff.

Nothing else happened
That day.

Nothing much, anyway,

But the eyeball in the crisps
Was enough.

Ian McMillan

Refugee

Sitting all alone
in a strange room
in a strange country
talking to a teddy bear
who can't understand
what I'm saying.

Adrian Henri

The Dragon's Birthday Party

It's the dragon's birthday party,
he's ten years old today.
'Come and do your special trick,'
I heard his mother say.

October

We crowded round the table,
we pushed and shoved to see
as someone brought the cake mix in
and the dragon laughed with glee.

It was just a bowl with flour in
and eggs and milk and that
with ten blue candles round the top
in the shape of Postman Pat.

The dragon took a big deep breath
stood up to his full size
and blew a blast of smoke and flame
that made us shut our eyes.

We felt the air grow hotter
we knew the taste of fear.
I felt a spark fly through the air
and land on my left ear.

But when we looked,
make no mistake:
the candles were lit
and the cake was baked.

Ian McMillan

Pencil and Paint

Winter has a pencil
For pictures clear and neat,
She traces the black tree-tops
Upon a snowy sheet.
But autumn has a palette
And a painting-brush instead,
And daubs the leaves for pleasure
With yellow, brown, and red.

Eleanor Farjeon

Little Red Riding Hood and the Wolf

As soon as Wolf began to feel
That he would like a decent meal,
He went and knocked on Grandma's door.
When Grandma opened it, she saw
The sharp white teeth, the horrid grin,
And Wolfie said, 'May I come in?'
Poor Grandmamma was terrified,
'He's going to eat me up!' she cried.
And she was absolutely right.
He ate her up in one big bite.
But Grandmamma was small and tough,
And Wolfie wailed, 'That's not enough!
I haven't yet begun to feel
That I have had a decent meal!'
He ran around the kitchen yelping,
'I've *got* to have another helping!'
Then added with a frightful leer,
'I'm therefore going to wait right here
Till Little Miss Red Riding Hood
Comes home from walking in the wood.'

He quickly put on Grandma's clothes,
(Of course he hadn't eaten those.)
He dressed himself in coat and hat.
He put on shoes and after that
He even brushed and curled his hair,
Then sat himself in Grandma's chair.
In came the little girl in red.
She stopped. She stared. And then she said,

'*What great big ears you have, Grandma.*'
'*All the better to hear you with,*' the Wolf replied.
'*What great big eyes you have, Grandma,*'
    said Little Red Riding Hood.
'*All the better to see you with,*' the Wolf replied.

He sat there watching her and smiled.
He thought, I'm going to eat this child.
Compared with her old Grandmamma
She's going to taste like caviar.

Then Little Red Riding Hood said, '*But Grandma,
what a lovely great big furry coat you have on.*'

'That's wrong!' cried Wolf. 'Have you forgot
To tell me what BIG TEETH I've got?
Ah well, no matter what you say,
I'm going to eat you anyway.'
The small girl smiles. One eyelid flickers.
She whips a pistol from her knickers.
She aims it at the creature's head
And *bang bang bang*, she shoots him dead.
A few weeks later, in the wood,
I came across Miss Riding Hood.
But what a change! No cloak of red,
No silly hood upon her head.
She said, 'Hello, and do please note
My lovely furry WOLFSKIN COAT.'

Roald Dahl

Rhinoceros

God simply got bored and started doodling
with ideas he'd given up on, scooping off the floor
bits and bobs and sticking them together:
the tail of a ten-ton pig he'd meant for Norway,
the long skull of a too-heavy dinosaur,
the armour plating of his first version of
the hippo, an unpainted beak of a toucan
stuck on back to front, a dash of tantrums
he intended for the Abyssinian owl, the same
awful grey colour he'd used for landscaping the moon.

And tempted to try it with the batteries,
he set it down on the wild plains of Africa,
grinned at what he saw and let it run.

Matt Simpson

Five Little Owls

Five little owls in an old elm-tree,
Fluffy and puffy as owls could be,
Blinking and winking with big round eyes
At the big round moon that hung in the skies:
As I passed beneath, I could hear one say,
'There'll be mouse for supper, there will, today!'
Then all of them hooted, 'Tu-whit, Tu-whoo!
Yes, mouse for supper, Hoo hoo, Hoo hoo!'

Anon.

Two Witches Discuss Good Grooming

'How do you keep your teeth so green
Whilst mine remain quite white?
Although I rub them vigorously
With cold slime every night.

Your eyes are such a lovely shade
Of bloodshot, streaked with puce.
I prod mine daily with a stick
But it isn't any use.

I envy so, the spots and boils
That brighten your complexion
Even rat spit on my face
Left no trace of infection.

I've even failed to have bad breath
After eating sewage raw,
Yet your halitosis
Can strip paint from a door.'

'My dear, there is no secret,
Now I don't mean to brag.
What you see is nature's work
I'm just a natural hag.'

John Coldwell

November

from *The Lady of Shalott*

I

On either side the river lie
Long fields of barley and of rye,
That clothe the wold and meet the sky;
And thro' the field the road runs by
        To many-tower'd Camelot;
And up and down the people go,
Gazing where the lilies blow
Round an island there below,
        The island of Shalott.

Willows whiten, aspens quiver,
Little breezes dusk and shiver
Thro' the wave that runs for ever
By the island in the river
    Flowing down to Camelot.
Four gray walls, and four gray towers,
Overlook a space of flowers,
And the silent isle imbowers
    The Lady of Shalott.

By the margin, willow-veil'd,
Slide the heavy barges trail'd
By slow horses; and unhail'd
The shallop flitteth silken-sail'd
    Skimming down to Camelot:
But who hath seen her wave her hand?
Or at the casement seen her stand?
Or is she known in all the land,
    The Lady of Shalott?

Only reapers, reaping early
In among the bearded barley,
Hear a song that echoes cheerly
From the river winding clearly,
    Down to tower'd Camelot:
And by the moon the reaper weary,
Piling sheaves in uplands airy,
Listening, whispers, ''Tis the fairy
    Lady of Shalott.'

II

There she weaves by night and day
A magic web with colours gay.
She has heard a whisper say,
A curse is on her if she stay
    To look down to Camelot.
She knows not what the curse may be,
And so she weaveth steadily,
And little other care hath she,
    The Lady of Shalott.

And moving thro' a mirror clear
That hangs before her all the year,
Shadows of the world appear.
There she sees the highway near
    Winding down to Camelot:
There the river eddy whirls,
And there the surly village-churls,
And the red cloaks of market girls,
    Pass onward from Shalott.

Sometimes a troop of damsels glad,
An abbot on an ambling pad,
Sometimes a curly shepherd-lad,
Or long-hair'd page in crimson clad,
    Goes by to tower'd Camelot;
And sometimes thro' the mirror blue
The knights come riding two and two:
She hath no loyal knight and true,
    The Lady of Shalott.

But in her web she still delights
To weave the mirror's magic sights,
For often thro' the silent nights
A funeral, with plumes and lights,
    And music, went to Camelot:
Or when the moon was overhead,
Came two young lovers lately wed;
'I am half sick of shadows,' said
    The Lady of Shalott.

Alfred Lord Tennyson

The Pet Wig

Our teacher has a pet wig,
Nobody knows its name,
It clings to his baldy head
And looks extremely tame.

It's very calm and patient.
When dogs are on the prowl
It pretends it cannot hear the way
They clear their throats and growl.

It comes from a far-off land
(Or so we like to think),
A strange endangered species
That's just about extinct.

After school he takes it off
And offers it some milk.
He strokes it extra gently
(Its fur is smooth as silk).

And in his lonely room at night
When he decides to retire,
He lays it down quite carefully
On a blanket near the fire.

After a long day clinging,
It rests content and purring.

Brian Patten

November Returns

Firework time, and this year, gales.
Large trees dip and bow tearing their leaves
Against the air, which seems to thicken now.
Not a quiet time even when the weather is quiet.
Fireworks, and your birthday: the year beginning
Apart from the calendar. A time when things have
   happened.
Advenire, Advent: to come to reach to happen.

November

Some years there is sunshine pale in woods.
It lies in splashes like paint on leaves, on the track,
A pausing in the year before it swings
Down to the dark,
And the leaves thin – beech-gold, pebble-brown
A clearing in the grove.
On some dim soft dun afternoon
Having to wait for something, you go a stroll
At the back of the works ('back in twenty minutes').
An astounding tree picked out by secret sunshine
Makes sense of the Golden Bough, the magic in woods.

Bonfires, Hallowe'en past, children running through streets,
Something stirring in the blood that makes us rise
And stand at the window, leaving the curtain ajar,
Expectant of something, watching, waiting
For something to happen; someone, perhaps, to arrive.
Maybe it is just the wind shifting direction
Dropping leaves at doors, pattering rain on the windows.

I draw the curtains, light the fire, for you
And others I have lit for at this time:
Ghosts returning to their winter quarters
To keep me company, to celebrate the season.

Jenny Joseph

Starlight, Starbright

Starlight,
Starbright.
First star I see tonight,
I wish I may,
I wish I might,
Have this wish I wish tonight.

Anon.

The Bonfire at Barton Point

The bonfire at Barton Point
was a wonderful sight, a spectacular blaze,
stuff legends are made of, wicked, ace,
we were talking about it for days.

There were beehives, signboards, slats and tables,
car tyres, a sledge and a wrecked go-cart,
a radiogram with a case of records,
some put-together furniture that must have pulled apart.

And like patients forsaken in mid-operation
there were three-piece suites in states of distress,
gashes in sides, stuffing pulled out,
and a huge Swiss roll of a mattress.

And we knew we'd need some giant of a guy
to lord it over a pile like this,
not a wimp in a baby's pushchair
that the flames would quickly dismiss.

But on the great and glorious night
we found it hard to believe our eyes
as tilted and tumbled onto the fire
came a whole procession of guys.

Then adults took over and just to ensure
the pile of guys would really burn,
they doused the heap with paraffin
so no ghost of a guy could return.

Then matches flared, torches were lit
at several points around the fire
till suddenly everything caught at once
and fingers of flame reached higher.

And beaming guys still peered through smoke
till the fiery serpent wrapped them round
in coils of flame, and they toppled down
to merge with the blazing mound.

With our faces scorched, we turned away,
driven back by waves of heat
till after a time the fire slumped back,
its appetite replete.

Now as long as we live we'll remember
Barton Point with its fiery display
and the charred and blackened treasures
that we pulled from the ashes next day.

Brian Moses

Sonnet 73

That time of year thou mayst in me behold
When yellow leaves, or none, or few, do hang
Upon those boughs which shake against the cold,
Bare ruin'd choirs where late the sweet birds sang.
In me thou see'st the twilight of such day
As after sunset fadeth in the west,
Which by and by black night doth take away,
Death's second self, that seals up all in rest.
In me thou see'st the glowing of such fire,
That on the ashes of his youth doth lie,
As the death-bed whereon it must expire,
Consum'd with that which it was nourish'd by.
  This thou perceiv'st, which makes thy love more strong,
  To love that well which thou must leave ere long.

William Shakespeare

Divali

Winter stalks us
like a leopard in the mountains
scenting prey.

It grows dark,
bare trees stick black bars
across the moon's silver eye.

I will light my lamp for you
Lakshmi,
drive away the darkness.

Welcome you into my home
Lakshmi,
beckon you from every window

With light that blazes
out like flames
across the sombre sky.

Certain houses
crouch in shadow, do not hear
your gentle voice.

Will not feel
your gentle heartbeat
bring prosperity and fortune.

Darkness hunts them
like a leopard in the mountains
stalking prey.

David Harmer

You'd Better Believe Him
A Fable

Discovered an old rocking-horse in Woolworth's,
He tried to feed it but without much luck
So he stroked it, had a long conversation about
The trees it came from, the attics it had visited.
Tried to take it out then
But the store detective he
Called the police who in court next morning said
'He acted strangely when arrested,
His statement read simply "I believe in rocking-horses."
We have no reason to believe him mad.'
'Quite so,' said the prosecution,
'Bring in the rocking-horse as evidence.'
'I'm afraid it's escaped, sir,' said the store manager,
'Left a hoof print as evidence
On the skull of the store detective.'
'Quite so,' said the prosecution, fearful
Of the neighing
Out in the corridor.

Brian Patten

Inversnaid

This darksome burn, horseback brown,
His rollrock highroad roaring down,
In coop and in comb the fleece of his foam
Flutes and low to the lake falls home.

A windpuff-bonnet of fawn-froth
Turns and twindles over the broth
Of a pool so pitchblack, fell frowning,
It rounds and rounds Despair to drowning.

Degged with dew, dappled with dew
Are the groins of the braes that the brook treads through,
Wiry heathpacks, flitches of fern,
And the beadbonny ash that sits over the burn.

What would the world be, once bereft
Of wet and of wildness? Let them be left,
O let them be left, wildness and wet;
Long live the weeds and the wilderness yet.

Gerard Manley Hopkins

Typo

'Nitgub,' said the typewriter,
and clenched the paper tight.
'Nitgub positively.
It is here in black and white.'
'Nonsense,' I said.
'I typed N-O-T-H-I-N-G;
the word of course was *nothing*,
simply nothing, don't you see?'
'Nothing may be what you meant,
but *nitgub*'s what you wrote.
I like it,' said the typewriter.
'It strikes a happy note.
It has more style than *nothing*,
has a different sort of sound.
The colour is superior;
the flavour's nice and round.
Have you plumbed its deepest depths,
its mystery explained?'
'All right,' I said, 'I'll take it.
Nitgub ventured, nitgub gained.'

Russell Hoban

Anthem for Doomed Youth

What passing-bells for these who die as cattle?
　– Only the monstrous anger of the guns.
　Only the stuttering rifles' rapid rattle
Can patter out their hasty orisons.
No mockeries now for them; no prayers nor bells,
　Nor any voice of mourning save the choirs, –
The shrill, demented choirs of wailing shells;
　And bugles calling for them from sad shires.

What candles may be held to speed them all?
　Not in the hands of boys but in their eyes
Shall shine the holy glimmers of goodbyes.
　The pallor of girls' brows shall be their pall;
Their flowers the tenderness of patient minds,
And each slow dusk a drawing-down of blinds.

Wilfred Owen

The Old Wife and the Ghost

There was an old wife and she lived all alone
   In a cottage not far from Hitchin:
And one bright night, by the full moon light,
   Comes a ghost right into her kitchen.

About that kitchen neat and clean
   The ghost goes pottering round.
But the poor old wife is deaf as a boot
   And so hears never a sound.

The ghost blows up the kitchen fire,
   As bold as bold can be;
He helps himself from the larder shelf,
   But never a sound hears she.

He blows on his hands to make them warm,
   And whistles aloud 'Whee-hee!'
But still as a sack the old soul lies
   And never a sound hears she.

November

From corner to corner he runs about,
    And into the cupboard he peeps;
He rattles the door and bumps on the floor,
    But still the old wife sleeps.

Jangle and bang go the pots and pans,
    As he throws them all around;
And the plates and mugs and dishes and jugs,
    He flings them all to the ground.

Madly the ghost tears up and down
    And screams like a storm at sea;
And at last the old wife stirs in her bed –
    And it's 'Drat those mice,' says she.

Then the first cock crows and morning shows
    And the troublesome ghost's away.
But oh! what a pickle the poor wife sees
    When she gets up next day.

'Them's tidy big mice,' the old wife thinks,
    And off she goes to Hitchin,
And a tidy big cat she fetches back
    To keep the mice from her kitchen.

James Reeves

Body Talk

Dere's a Sonnet
Under me bonnet
Dere's a Epic
In me ear,
Dere's a Novel
In me navel
Dere's a Classic
Here somewhere.
Dere's a Movie
In me left knee
A long story
In me right,
Dere's a shorty
Inbetweeny
It is tickly
In de night.
Dere's a picture
In me ticker
Unmixed riddims
In me heart,
In me texture
Dere's a comma
In me fat chin
Dere is Art.

Dere's an Opera
In me bladder
A Ballad's
In me wrist
Dere is laughter
In me shoulder
In me guzzard's
A nice twist.
In me dreadlocks
Dere is syntax
A dance kicks
In me bum
Thru me blood tracks
Dere run true facts
I got limericks
From me Mum,
Documentaries
In me entries
Plays on history
In me folk,
Dere's a Trilogy
When I tink of three
On me toey
Dere's a joke.

Benjamin Zephaniah

November

The leaves are fading and falling,
   The winds are rough and wild,
The birds have ceased their calling,
   But let me tell you, my child,

Though day by day, as it closes,
   Doth darker and colder grow,
The roots of the bright red roses
   Will keep alive in the snow.

And when the Winter is over,
   The boughs will get new leaves,
The quail come back to the clover,
   And the swallow back to the eaves.

The robin will wear on his bosom
   A vest that is bright and new,
And the loveliest way-side blossom
   Will shine with the sun and dew.

November

The leaves today are whirling,
    The brooks are dry and dumb,
But let me tell you, my darling,
    The Spring will be sure to come.

There must be rough, cold weather,
    And winds and rains so wild;
Not all good things together
    Come to us here, my child.

So, when some dear joy loses
    Its beauteous summer glow,
Think how the roots of the roses
    Are kept alive in the snow.

Alice Cary

As I Walked Out One Night

As I walked out one night, it being dark all over,
The moon did show no light I could discover,
Down by a river-side where ships were sailing,
A lonely maid I spied, weeping and bewailing.

I boldly stept up to her, and asked what grieved her,
She made this reply, None could relieve her,
'For my love is pressed,' she cried, 'to cross the ocean,
My mind is like the Sea, always in motion.'

He said, 'My pretty fair maid, mark well my story,
For your true love and I fought for England's glory,
By one unlucky shot we both got parted,
And by the wounds he got, I'm broken hearted.

'He told me before he died, his heart was broken,
He gave me this gold ring, take it for a token, –
"Take this unto my dear, there is no one fairer,
Tell her to be kind and love the bearer."'

Soon as these words he spoke she ran distracted,
Not knowing what she did, nor how she acted,
She run ashore, her hair showing her anger,
'Young man, you've come too late, for I'll wed no stranger.'

Soon as these words she spoke, his love grew stronger,
He flew into her arms, he could wait no longer,
They both sat down and sung, but she sung clearest,
Like a nightingale in spring, 'Welcome home, my dearest.'

He sang, 'God bless the wind that blew him over.'
She sang, 'God bless the ship that brought him over.'
They both sat down and sung but she sung clearest,
Like a nightingale in spring, 'Welcome home, my dearest.'

Anon.

Autumn

I love the fitful gust that shakes
    The casement all the day,
And from the glossy elm tree takes
    The faded leaves away,
Twirling them by the window pane
With thousand others down the lane.

I love to see the shaking twig
    Dance till shut of eve,
The sparrow on the cottage rig,
    Whose chirp would make believe
That Spring was just now flirting by
In Summer's lap with flowers to lie.

I love to see the cottage smoke
    Curl upwards through the trees;
The pigeons nestled round the cote
    On November days like these;
The cock upon the dunghill crowing,
The mill sails on the heath a-going.

John Clare

When You Are Old

When you are old and grey and full of sleep,
And nodding by the fire, take down this book,
And slowly read, and dream of the soft look
Your eyes had once, and of their shadows deep;

How many loved your moments of glad grace,
And loved your beauty with love false or true,
But one man loved the pilgrim soul in you,
And loved the sorrows of your changing face;

And bending down beside the glowing bars,
Murmur, a little sadly, how Love fled
And paced upon the mountains overhead
And hid his face amid a crowd of stars.

W.B. Yeats

A Night I had Trouble Falling Asleep

I stayed over at Eliot's house.
'I've lost my pet,' he said.
'So please wake me up in the middle of the night
If you find a big snake in your bed.'

Jeff Moss

Wanted – A Witch's Cat

Wanted – a witch's cat.
Must have vigor and spite,
Be expert at hissing,
And good in a fight,
And have balance and poise
On a broomstick at night.

November

Wanted – a witch's cat.
Must have hypnotic eyes
To tantalize victims
And mesmerize spies,
And be an adept
At scanning the skies.

Wanted – a witch's cat,
With a sly, cunning smile,
A knowledge of spells
And a good deal of guile,
With a fairly hot temper
And plenty of bile.

Wanted – a witch's cat,
Who's not afraid to fly,
For a cat with strong nerves
The salary's high.
Wanted – a witch's cat;
Only the best need apply.

Shelagh McGee

The Wind

Listen to the wind awailing
Rattling the garden gate
Brushing the leaves of the oak tree
Rustling in the grate.

The cat lies flat on the hearth rug
Washing his face with his paws
The dog's asleep in the basket
Everyone's indoors.

It screams along the alleys
It bellows up the street
It groans between the gravestones
It bowls hats along the street.

It's pounding at the windows
Like the hooves of an angry horse
If it blows like this much longer
It'll knock the world off its course.

November

It's quietened down at bedtime
Snoring loud and deep
At six it rattles the milk crates
And finally falls asleep.

Gareth Owen

A Dog's Life

I don't like being me sometimes,
   slumped here
on the carpet, cocking my ears
   every time
someone shuffles or shifts their feet,
   thinking
could be going walkies or getting grub
   or allowed to see
if the cat's left more than a smell
   on her plate.
She's never refused, that cat! Sometimes
   I find myself
dreaming (twitching my eyes, my fur)
   of being just
say *half* as canny as her, with her pert miaow,
   her cheeky tail
flaunting! These people sprawled
   in armchairs
gawping at telly, why don't they play ball
   with me
or enjoy a good nose-licking, eh?

Matt Simpson

Henry King,

Who chewed bits of String, and was early cut off in Dreadful Agonies.

The Chief Defect of Henry King
Was chewing little bits of String.
At last he swallowed some which tied
Itself in ugly Knots inside.
Physicians of the Utmost Fame
Were called at once; but when they came
They answered, as they took their Fees,
'There is no Cure for this Disease.
Henry will very soon be dead.'
His Parents stood about his Bed
Lamenting his Untimely Death,
When Henry, with his Latest Breath,
Cried – 'Oh, my Friends, be warned by me,
That Breakfast, Dinner, Lunch and Tea
Are all the Human Frame requires . . .'
With that the Wretched Child expires.

Hilaire Belloc

412

The Song of the Jellicles

Jellicle Cats come out to-night
Jellicle Cats come one come all:
The Jellicle Moon is shining bright –
Jellicles come to the Jellicle Ball.

Jellicle Cats are black and white,
Jellicle Cats are rather small;
Jellicle Cats are merry and bright,
And pleasant to hear when they caterwaul.
Jellicle Cats have cheerful faces,
Jellicle Cats have bright black eyes;
They like to practise their airs and graces
And wait for the Jellicle Moon to rise.

Jellicle Cats develop slowly,
Jellicle Cats are not too big;
Jellicle Cats are roly-poly,
They know how to dance a gavotte and a jig.
Until the Jellicle Moon appears
They make their toilette and take their repose:
Jellicles wash behind their ears,
Jellicles dry between their toes.

Jellicle Cats are white and black,
Jellicle Cats are of moderate size;
Jellicles jump like a jumping-jack;
Jellicle Cats have moonlit eyes.
They're quiet enough in the morning hours,
They're quiet enough in the afternoon,
Reserving their terpsichorean powers
To dance by the light of the Jellicle Moon.

Jellicle Cats are black and white,
Jellicle Cats (as I said) are small;
If it happens to be a stormy night
They will practise a caper or two in the hall.
If it happens the sun is shining bright
You would say they had nothing to do at all:
They are resting and saving themselves to be right
For the Jellicle moon and the Jellicle Ball.

T.S. Eliot

Thumbprint

On the pad of my thumb
are whorls, whirls, wheels
in a unique design:
mine alone.
What a treasure to own!
My own flesh, my own feelings.
No other, however grand or base,
can ever contain the same.
My signature,
thumbing the pages of my time.
My universe key,
my singularity.
Impress, implant,
I am myself,
of all my atom parts I am the sum.
And out of my blood and my brain
I make my own interior weather,
my own sun and rain.
Imprint my mark upon the world
whatever I shall become.

Eve Merriam

What For!

One more word, said my dad,
And I'll give you what for.

What for? I said.

That's right, he said, what for!

No, I said, I mean what for?
What will you give me what for for?

Never you mind, he said. Wait and see.

But what is what for for? I said.

What's what for for? he said,
It's to teach you what's what,
That's what.

What's that? I said.

Right, he said, you're for it,
I'm going to let you have it.

Have what? I said.

Have what? he said,
What for, that's what.
Do you want me to really give you
Something to think about?

I don't know, I said,
I'm thinking about it.

Then he clipped me over the ear.

It was the first time he'd made sense
All day.

Noel Petty

26

A Poem with Two Lauras In It

'Laura. Is that you?'
'Yes, Laura. It's me.'
'Where are we?'
'We're caught inside some sort of
three verse poem.'
'POEM!'
'Look out. Here comes the second verse.
Jump!'

'Made it.'
'Now that we're in this poem, what do we do?'
'Maybe we should rhyme for a bit.'
'We'd have to find the words to fit.'
'Good. That worked. Think of something, Laura.'
'My jumper. It's made from angora.'
'Phew. Lucky you weren't wearing your sweatshirt.'
'Mum wouldn't let me. It was covered with dirt.'
'I wish this verse would come to an end.'
'This rhyming is driving me round the bed.'
'Look below you. It's verse number three.'
'I'll go first. You follow me.'

'That was a near thing. I'm exhausted.'
'Me too. Let's rest on this long line until the poem comes to
    an end.'

John Coldwell

You must never bath in an Irish Stew

You must never bath in an Irish Stew
It's a most illogical thing to do
   But should you persist against my reasoning
   Don't fail to add the appropriate seasoning.

Spike Milligan

Never Since Eden

The Thing that came from Outer Space
And landed in the Jones' backyard
Had neither colour, size nor shape,
But a smell that caught us all off guard.

Never since Eden had there been
So sweet, so rich, so good a smell:
The neighbours, sniffing, gathered round
Like thirsting cattle at a well.

Never since Adam first kissed Eve
Had humans looked upon each other
With such joy that old enemies
Threw loving arms round one another

One whiff, and babies stopped their crying,
And all the gossip was kind and good,
And thieves and thugs and hooligans
Danced in the street in holiday mood.

Old scores were settled with a smile,
And liars changed to honest men,
And the ugliest face was beautiful,
And the sick and infirm were made whole again.

November

The Thing that came from Outer Space
Purred like a cat at the heart of the smell,
But *how* it did, and *why* it did,
Was more than the Scientists could tell.

They roped it off, they cleared the streets,
They closed upon it, wearing masks,
Ringed it with Geiger counters, scooped
And sealed it in aseptic flasks.

They took it back to analyse
In laboratories white and bare,
And they proved with burette and chromatograph
That nothing whatever was there.

They sterilized the Jones' backyard
(The smell whimpered and died without trace),
Then they showed by mathematics that no Thing
Could have landed from Outer Space.

So the neighbours are quite their old selves now,
As loving as vipers or stoats,
Cheating and lying and waiting their chance
To leap at each other's throats.

Raymond Wilson

Greedy Dog

This dog will eat anything.

Apple cores and bacon fat,
Milk you poured out for the cat.
He likes the string that ties the roast
And relishes hot buttered toast.
Hide your chocolates! He's a thief,
He'll even eat your handkerchief.
And if you don't like sudden shocks,
Carefully conceal your socks.
Leave some soup without a lid,
And you'll wish you never did.
When you think he must be full,
You find him gobbling bits of wool,
Orange peel or paper bags,
Dusters and old cleaning rags.

This dog will eat anything,
Except for mushrooms and cucumber.

Now what is wrong with those, I wonder?

James Hurley

Skimbleshanks: The Railway Cat

There's a whisper down the line at 11.39
When the Night Mail's ready to depart,
Saying 'Skimble where is Skimble has he gone to hunt the
  thimble?
We must find him or the train can't start.'
All the guards and all the porters and the stationmaster's
  daughters
They are searching high and low,
Saying 'Skimble where is Skimble for unless he's very nimble
Then the Night Mail just can't go.'
At 11.42 then the signal's nearly due
And the passengers are frantic to a man –
Then Skimble will appear and he'll saunter to the rear:
He's been busy in the luggage van!
  He gives one flash of his glass-green eyes
    And the signal goes 'All Clear!'
  And we're off at last for the northern part
    Of the Northern Hemisphere!

You may say that by and large it is Skimble who's in charge
Of the Sleeping Car Express.
From the driver and the guards to the bagmen playing cards
He will supervise them all, more or less.
Down the corridor he paces and examines all the faces
Of the travellers in the First and in the Third;
He establishes control by a regular patrol
And he'd know at once if anything occurred.
He will watch you without winking and he sees what you
    are thinking
And it's certain that he doesn't approve
Of hilarity and riot, so the folk are very quiet
When Skimble is about and on the move.
    You can play no pranks with Skimbleshanks!
        He's a Cat that cannot be ignored;
    So nothing goes wrong on the Northern Mail
        When Skimbleshanks is aboard.

Oh it's very pleasant when you have found your little den
With your name written up on the door.
And the berth is very neat with a newly folded sheet
And there's not a speck of dust on the floor.
There is every sort of light – you can make it dark or bright;
There's a button that you turn to make a breeze.
There's a funny little basin you're supposed to wash your
    face in
And a crank to shut the window if you sneeze.
Then the guard looks in politely and will ask you very
    brightly
'Do you like your morning tea weak or strong?'
But Skimble's just behind him and was ready to remind him,
For Skimble won't let anything go wrong.
    And when you creep into your cosy berth
        And pull up the counterpane,
You are bound to admit that it's very nice
To know that you won't be bothered by mice –
You can leave all that to the Railway Cat,
    The Cat of the Railway Train!

In the middle of the night he is always fresh and bright;
Every now and then he has a cup of tea
With perhaps a drop of Scotch while he's keeping on the
    watch,
Only stopping here and there to catch a flea.
You were fast asleep at Crewe and so you never knew
That he was walking up and down the station;
You were sleeping all the while he was busy at Carlisle,
Where he greets the stationmaster with elation.
But you saw him at Dumfries, where he summons the police
If there's anything they ought to know about:
When you get to Gallowgate there you do not have to wait –
For Skimbleshanks will help you to get out!
  He gives you a wave of his long brown tail
    Which says: 'I'll see you again!
  You'll meet without fail on the Midnight Mail
    The Cat of the Railway Train.'

T.S. Eliot

December

A Wish

I wish I were a little bird
   That out of sight doth soar;
I wish I were a song once heard
   But often pondered o'er,
Or shadow of a lily stirred
   By wind upon the floor,
Or echo of a loving word
   Worth all that went before,
Or memory of a hope deferred
   That springs again no more.

Christina Rossetti

Tweedledum and Tweedledee

Tweedledum and Tweedledee
  Agreed to have a battle;
For Tweedledum said Tweedledee
  Had spoiled his nice new rattle.

Just then flew down a monstrous crow,
  As black as a tar-barrel;
Which frightened both the heroes so,
  They quite forgot their quarrel.

Anon.

The Late Passenger

The sky was low, the sounding rain was falling dense and
   dark,
And Noah's sons were standing at the window of the Ark.

The beasts were in, but Japhet said, 'I see one creature more
Belated and unmated there come knocking at the door.'

'Well let him knock,' said Ham, 'Or let him drown or learn
   to swim.
We're overcrowded as it is; we've got no room for him.'

'And yet it knocks, how terribly it knocks,' said Shem, 'Its
   feet
Are hard as horn – but oh the air that comes from it is
   sweet.'

'Now hush,' said Ham, 'You'll waken Dad, and once he
   comes to see
What's at the door, it's sure to mean more work for you and
   me.'

Noah's voice came roaring from the darkness down below,
'Some animal is knocking. Take it in before we go.'

Ham shouted back, and savagely he nudged the other two,
'That's only Japhet knocking down a brad-nail in his shoe.'

Said Noah, 'Boys, I hear a noise that's like a horse's hoof.'
Said Ham, 'Why, that's the dreadful rain that drums upon
   the roof.'

Noah tumbled up on deck and out he put his head;
His face went grey, his knees were loosed, he tore his beard
   and said,

'Look, look! It would not wait. It turns away. It takes its
   flight.
Fine work you've made of it, my sons, between you all
   tonight!

'Even if I could outrun it now, it would not turn again
– Not now. Our great discourtesy has earned its high
   disdain.

'Oh noble and unmated beast, my sons were all unkind;
In such a night what stable and what manger will you find?

'Oh golden hoofs, oh cataracts of mane, oh nostrils wide
With indignation! Oh the neck wave-arched, the lovely
   pride!

'Oh long shall be the furrows ploughed across the hearts of
    men
Before it comes to stable and to manger once again,

'And dark and crooked all the ways in which our race shall
    walk,
And shrivelled all their manhood like a flower with broken
    stalk,

'And all the world, oh Ham, may curse the hour when you
    were born
Because of you the Ark must sail without the Unicorn.'

C.S. Lewis

Silverly

Silverly,
  Silverly,
Over the
  Trees
The moon drifts
  By on a
Runaway
  Breeze.

Dozily,
  Dozily,
Deep in her
  Bed,
A little girl
  Dreams with the
Moon in her
  Head.

Dennis Lee

Desk

It was stuffy in the classroom.
He put his hand inside his desk,
Feeling for a pencil. It was cool in there,
He let his hand swing aimlessly around.
The space within seemed vast, and when
He reached in further he found
Nothing, could feel no books, no ruler.
His hand floated as if in a bath of shadows,
Airy and refreshing, not at all
The same place that the rest of him was in.

He put both hands in, let them drift
Deeper, this way and that. It was more than empty,
The inside had no sides. His hands
Never reappeared through some unexpected hole.
He lifted the lid quietly a little more. A waft
Of soft air cooled his face, the same
As on summer nights or under leafy trees.

He bent his head down to the gap. He looked inside.
Dark as deep water, deep as a clear night sky.
He smiled. He put his head inside.
'What are you doing?' asked the teacher. But he didn't hear.
He slid his shoulders in, and then
Before anyone could reach to stop him,
He bent from the waist, kicking his chair back,
And with a muffled cry of pleasure
Dived. For a split second,
As the room filled with fresh air,
We watched his legs slide slowly down into the desk
And disappear. And then the lid fell back,
Shut, with a soft thud.

Dave Calder

Snow and Ice Poems

(i)   Our street is dead lazy
      especially in winter.
      Some mornings you wake up
      and it's still lying there
      saying nothing. Huddled
      under its white counterpane.

      But soon the lorries arrive
      like angry mums,
      pull back the blankets
      and send it shivering
      off to work.

(ii) To
      boggan?
      or not
      to boggan?
      That is the question.

(iii)   Winter
morning.
Snowflakes
for breakfast.
The street
outside
quiet
as a
long
white
bandage.

(iv)   The time I like best
is 6 a.m.
and the snow is six inches deep

Which I'm yet to discover
'cos I'm under the cover
and fast, fast asleep.

Roger McGough

Love-light

A taper lit in sunlight,
Pale yellow leaf of flame,
An upturned heart that trembled
As soft winds breathed your name,
Its brightness was diluted;
But, when the darkness came,
It shone with such pure brilliance
As put the stars to shame.

Vernon Scannell

Furry Bear

If I were a bear
    And a big bear too,
I shouldn't much care
    If it froze or snew;
I wouldn't much mind
    If it snowed or friz –
I'd be all fur-lined
    With a coat like his!

For I'd have fur boots and a brown fur wrap,
And brown fur knickers and a big fur cap.
I'd have a fur muffle-ruff to cover my jaws,
And, brown fur mittens on my big brown paws.
With a big brown furry-down up on my head,
I'd sleep all winter in a big fur bed.

A.A. Milne

The Computer's First Christmas Card

jollymerry
hollyberry
jollyberry
merryholly
happyjolly
jollyjelly
jellybelly
bellymerry
hollyheppy
jollyMolly
marryJerry
merryHarry
happyBarry
heppyJarry
boppyheppy
berryjorry
jorryjolly
moppyjelly
Mollymerry
Jerryjolly
bellyboppy
jorryhoppy
hollymoppy

December

Barrymerry
Jarryhappy
happyboppy
boppyjolly
jollymerry
merrymerry
merrymerry
merryChris
ammerryasa
Chrismerry
asMERRYCHR
YSANTHEMUM

Edwin Morgan

Small, Smaller

I thought that I knew all there was to know
Of being small, until I saw once, black against the snow,
A shrew, trapped in my footprint, jump and fall
And jump again and fall, the hole too deep, the walls too
   tall.

Russell Hoban

Nobody Rides the Unicorn

His coat is like snowflakes
Woven with silk.
When he goes galloping
He flows like milk.

His life is all gentle
And his heart is bold.
His single horn is magical
Barley sugar gold.

Nobody rides the Unicorn
As he grazes under a secret sun.
His understanding is so great
That he forgives us, every one.

Nobody rides the Unicorn,
His mind is peaceful as the grass.
He is the loveliest one of all
And he sleeps behind the waterfall.

Adrian Mitchell

An Attempt at Unrhymed Verse

People tell you all the time,
Poems do not have to rhyme.
It's often better if they don't
And I'm determined this one won't.
                                  Oh dear.

Never mind, I'll start again.
Busy, busy with my pen . . . cil.
I can do it if I try –
Easy, peasy, pudding and gherkins.

Writing verse is so much fun,
Cheering as the summer weather,
Makes you feel alert and bright,
'Specially when you get it more or less the way you want it.

Wendy Cope

Given an Apple

He brought her an apple. She would not eat
And he was hurt until she said,
'I'm keeping it as a charm. It may
Grow small and wrinkled. I don't care.
I'll always think of you today.
Time is defeated for that hour
When you gave me an apple for
A love token, and more.'

Elizabeth Jennings

Nine Mice

Nine mice on tiny tricycles
went riding on the ice,
they rode in spite of warning signs,
they rode despite advice.

The signs were right, the ice was thin,
in half a trice, the mice fell in,
and from their chins down to their toes,
those mice entirely froze.

Nine mindless mice, who paid the price,
are thawing slowly by the ice,
still sitting on their tricycles
. . . nine white and shiny *micicles!*

Jack Prelutsky

little tree

little tree
little silent Christmas tree
you are so little
you are more like a flower

who found you in the green forest
and were you very sorry to come away?
see   i will comfort you
because you smell so sweetly

i will kiss your cool bark
and hug you safe and tight
just as your mother would,
only don't be afraid

look   the spangles
that sleep all the year in a dark box
dreaming of being taken out and allowed to shine,
the balls the chains red and gold the fluffy threads,

put up your little arms
and i'll give them all to you to hold
every finger shall have its ring
and there won't be a single place dark or unhappy

then when you're quite dressed
you'll stand in the window for everyone to see
and how they'll stare!
oh but you'll be very proud

and my little sister and i will take hands
and looking up at our beautiful tree
we'll dance and sing
'Noel Noel'

e.e. cummings

Just Before Christmas

Down the Holloway Road on the top of the bus
On the just-before-Christmas nights we go,
Allie and me and all of us,
And we look at the lit-up shops below.
Orange and yellow the fruit stalls glow,
Store windows are sploshed with sort-of-snow,
And Santa's a poor old so-and-so,
With his sweating gear and his sack in tow,
And Christ . . . mas is coming!

At the front of the top of the lit-up bus
Way down the Holloway Road we ride,
Allie and me and all of us,
And the butchers chop and lop with pride,
And the turkeys squat with their stuffing inside
By ropes of sausages soon to be fried,
And every door is open wide
As down the road we growl or glide
And Christ . . . mas is coming!

December

All at the front of the top of the bus,
Far down the Holloway Road we roar,
Allie and me and all of us,
And tellies are tinselled in every store,
With fairy lights over every door,
With glitter and crêpe inside, what's more,
And everyone seeming to say, 'For sure,
Christmas is coming as never before.'
Yes, Christ . . . mas is coming!

Kit Wright

Christmas is Here

When the fee-fees start to bloom
Purple and white,
When the days begin to be
Shorter than night,
When the poinsettia's leaves
Turn from green to red,
When the turkey in the coop
Starts to look well-fed,
When we dig the yellow yams,
And pick the gungo peas,
When the tall, white, cane-flags
Start waving in the breeze,
When oranges and tangerines
Start to fill the baskets
Of the people on their way
To the different markets,
When the fruits which have been dried
Are soaking in the wine,
When the fat green cho-chos hang
Heavy from the vine,
When we look out in the fields
To the red bulbs of sorrel,
When the pickled meats come out

From their place in the brine barrel,
When each meal contains a slice
Of avocado pear,
Then we know for certain that
Christmas time is here.

Valerie Bloom

They're Fetching in Ivy and Holly

'They're fetching in ivy and holly
And putting it this way and that.
I simply can't think of the reason,'
Said Si-Si the Siamese cat.

'They're pinning up lanterns and streamers.
There's mistletoe over the door.
They've brought in a tree from the garden.
I do wish I knew what it's for.

'It's covered with little glass candles
That go on and off without stop.
They've put it to stand in a corner
And tied up a fairy on top.

'They're stringing bright cars by the dozen
And letting them hang in a row.
Some people outside in the roadway
Are singing a song in the snow.

'I saw all the children write letters
And – I'm not at all sure this was wise –
They posted each one *up the chimney*.
I couldn't believe my own eyes.

'What on earth, in the middle of winter,
Does the family think it is at?
Won't somebody please come and tell me?'
Said Si-Si the Siamese cat.

Charles Causley

A Silly Thing to Do

When Father pulled a cracker
with silly Uncle Joe,
they pulled and pulled and struggled
– then Father just let go!

Poor Uncle Joe went flying,
he flew into the street
and entered into orbit
– still sitting in his seat!

You'll see him every Christmas,
he rises in the West.
Just east of Mars and Saturn
is where you'll see him best . . .

He circles earth twice monthly.
So give poor Joe a thought,
when you pull your Christmas crackers
and drink your Christmas port.

Peter Dixon

Jingle Bells

Dashing through the snow,
In a one-horse open sleigh;
O'er the fields we go,
Laughing all the way;
Bells on bob-tail ring,
Making spirits bright;
Oh what fun to ride and sing
A sleighing song tonight.

Jingle bells, jingle bells,
Jingle all the way;
Oh! What joy it is to ride
In a one-horse open sleigh.
Jingle bells, jingle bells,
Jingle all the way;
Oh! What joy it is to ride
In a one-horse open sleigh.

James Pierpont

In the Bleak Mid-Winter

In the bleak mid-winter
    Frosty wind made moan,
Earth stood hard as iron,
    Water like a stone;
Snow had fallen, snow on snow,
    Snow on snow,
In the bleak mid-winter
    Long ago.

Our God, Heaven cannot hold Him
    Nor earth sustain;
Heaven and earth shall flee away
    When he comes to reign:
In the bleak mid-winter
    A stable-place sufficed
The Lord God Almighty
    Jesus Christ.

Enough for Him, whom cherubim
  Worship night and day,
A breastful of milk
  And a mangerful of hay;
Enough for Him, whom angels
  Fall down before,
The ox and ass and camel
  Which adore.

Angels and archangels
  May have gathered there,
Cherubim and seraphim
  Thronged the air;
But only His mother
  In her maiden bliss
Worshipped the Beloved
  With a kiss.

What can I give Him.
  Poor as I am?
If I were a shepherd
  I would bring a lamb,
If I were a Wise Man
  I would do my part, –
Yet what I can I give Him,
  Give my heart.

Christina Rossetti

I Wish I'd Been Present at Christmas Past

I wish I'd been a shepherd
and heard the angels sing.
I wish I'd been to Bethlehem
and seen the Infant King.

I wish I'd been a wise man
at the stable bare
following the star with
gold, frankincense and myrrh.

I wish I'd been an animal
who shared my manger hay
with that special new born baby
on that first Christmas Day.

Paul Cookson

A Christmas Blessing

God bless the master of this house,
  The mistress also,
And all the little children
That round the table go;
And all your kin and kinsfolk,
  That dwell both far and near:
I wish you a Merry Christmas
  And a Happy New Year.

Anon.

This Year I Will Stay Awake

This year I will stay awake
all night long make no mistake.
On this Christmas Eve I'll keep
my eyes open, try to peep.
This year I won't drowse or dream
but be alert till Santa's been,
see just what he leaves and how
he fits down our chimney now,
how the presents all appear
hear the sleigh bells and reindeer.
This year I will not count sheep
but pretend to be asleep.
No catnaps or snoozing but I
won't drop off and get some shut-eye.

This year there will be no slumber
I won't let myself go under.
No forty winks or throwing zeds.
No blinking, kipping, heavy headszz . . .
This year I won't nod or doze
or let my heavy eyelids close.
This year I won't nod or doze
or let my heavy eyelids close
or let my heavy eyelids close
or let my he..avy eye..li..ds clo..se
or let my he..avy eye..liiids clo..zzzzzzzzzzzzzzzzzzzz

Paul Cookson

The First Christmas

It never snows at Christmas in that dry and dusty land.
Instead of freezing blizzards, there are palms and drifting
   sands,
and years ago a stable and a most unusual star
and three wise men who followed it, by camel, not by car,
while, sleepy on the quiet hills, a shepherd gave a cry.
He'd seen a crowd of angels in the silent starlit sky.
In the stable, ox and ass stood very still and calm
and gazed upon the baby, safe and snug, in Mary's arms.
And Joseph, lost in shadows, face lit by an oil lamp's glow
stood wondering, that first Christmas Day, two thousand
   years ago.

Marian Swinger

The Twelve Days of Christmas

The first day of Christmas my true love sent to me:
A partridge in a pear tree.

The second day of Christmas my true love sent to me:
Two turtle doves, and a partridge in a pear tree.

The third day of Christmas my true love sent to me:
Three French hens, two turtle doves, and a partridge in a
pear tree.

The fourth day of Christmas my true love sent to me:
Four colly birds, three French hens, two turtle doves, and a
partridge in a pear tree.

The fifth day of Christmas my true love sent to me:
Five gold rings, four colly birds, three French hens, two
turtle doves, and a partridge in a pear tree.

The sixth day of Christmas my true love sent to me:
Six geese a-laying, five gold rings, four colly birds, three
French hens, two turtle doves, and a partridge in a pear
tree.

The seventh day of Christmas my true love sent to me:
Seven swans a-swimming, six geese a-laying, five gold rings,
    four colly birds, three French hens, two turtle doves, and
    a partridge in a pear tree.

The eighth day of Christmas my true love sent to me:
Eight maids a-milking, seven swans a-swimming, six geese
    a-laying, five gold rings, four colly birds, three French
    hens, two turtle doves, and a partridge in a pear tree.

The ninth day of Christmas my true love sent to me:
Nine drummers drumming, eight maids a-milking, seven
    swans a-swimming, six geese a-laying, five gold rings, four
    colly birds, three French hens, two turtle doves, and a
    partridge in a pear tree.

The tenth day of Christmas my true love sent to me:
Ten pipers piping, nine drummers drumming, eight maids a-
    milking, seven swans a-swimming, six geese a-laying, five
    gold rings, four colly birds, three French hens, two turtle
    doves, and a partridge in a pear tree.

The eleventh day of Christmas my true love sent to me:
Eleven ladies dancing, ten pipers piping, nine drummers
    drumming, eight maids a-milking, seven swans a-
    swimming, six geese a-laying, five gold rings, four colly
    birds, three French hens, two turtle doves, and a partridge
    in a pear tree.

The twelfth day of Christmas my true love sent to me:
Twelve lords a-leaping, eleven ladies dancing, ten pipers
  piping, nine drummers drumming, eight maids a-milking,
  seven swans a-swimming, six geese a-laying, five gold
  rings, four colly birds, three French hens, two turtle
  doves, and a partridge in a pear tree.

Anon.

On the Thirteenth Day of Christmas My True Love Phoned Me Up . . .

Well, I suppose I should be grateful, you've obviously gone
to a lot of trouble and expense – or maybe off your head.
Yes, I did like the birds – the small ones anyway were fun
if rather messy, but now the hens have roosted on my bed
and the rest are nested on the wardrobe. It's hard to sleep
with all that cooing, let alone the cackling of the geese
whose eggs are everywhere, but mostly in a broken smelly
   heap
on the sofa. No, why should I mind? I can't get any peace
anywhere – the lounge is full of drummers thumping tom-
   toms
and sprawling lords crashed out from manic leaping. The
kitchen is crammed with cows and milkmaids and smells of
   a million stink-bombs
and enough sour milk to last a year. The pipers? I'd
   forgotten them –
they were no trouble, I paid them and they went. But I can't
   get rid
of these young ladies. They won't stop dancing or turn the
   music down
and they're always in the bathroom, squealing as they skid
across the flooded floor. No, I don't need a plumber round,

it's just the swans – where else can they swim? Poor things,
I think they're going mad, like me. When I went to wash my
hands one ate the soap, another swallowed the gold rings.
And the pear tree died. Too dry. So thanks for nothing,
love. Goodbye.

Dave Calder

Visiting Mrs Neverley

Old Mrs Neverley
came from Back There.
She sat in the sunshine
with frost in her hair.
I'll be going home soon, she said.
Never said where.

December

Sweet crumbly biscuits,
ghostly-grey tea
and her smile would be waiting.
She listened to me
and sometimes to someone else
I couldn't see

and when we fell silent
and couldn't say why
she glanced at the window.
She smiled at the sky.
Look! There, you missed it.
An angel passed by.

It was one of her stories.
She said, *I'm growing too.*
You grow up, I grow down.
She told lies, I knew.
Only, now that she's gone
nothing else quite seems true.

Philip Gross

What No Snow?

Why doesn't it snow?
It's winter, isn't it?
Then it's supposed to snow.
How else can you make snowmen,
Or fight each other with snowballs,
And slide down hills on sledges?
It's not fair, is it?
Soon it will be summer,
Then it'll just rain and rain for months.
Can't anyone tell me,
WHY DOESN'T IT SNOW?

Bill Boyle

Cottage

When I live in a Cottage
I shall keep in my Cottage
  Two different Dogs
  Three creamy Cows
  Four giddy Goats
  Five pewter Pots
  Six silver Spoons
  Seven busy Beehives
  Eight ancient Appletrees
  Nine red Rosebushes
  Ten teeming Teapots
  Eleven chirping Chickens
  Twelve cosy Cats with their kittenish Kittens
    and
  One blessèd Baby in a Basket.
That's what I'll have when I live in my Cottage.

Eleanor Farjeon

Good Riddance But Now What?

Come, children, gather round my knee;
Something is about to be.

Tonight's December thirty-first,
Something is about to burst.

The clock is crouching, dark and small,
Like a time bomb in the hall.

Hark! It's midnight, children dear.
Duck! Here comes another year.

Ogden Nash

Index of First Lines

Index of First Lines

Index of First Lines

Index of First Lines

Index of First Lines

Index of First Lines

Index of Poets

481

Index of Poets

Index of Poets

Acknowledgements

The publishers wish to thank the following for permission to use copyright material:

John Agard, 'The Hurt Boy and the Birds' and 'A Date With the Spring' from *Get Back Pimple* (1996) Viking, by permission of Caroline Sheldon Literary Agency on behalf of the author; and 'The Older the Violin the Sweeter the Tune' from *Say it Again, Granny*, The Bodley Head, by permission of Random House UK Ltd; **Allan Ahlberg**, 'Glenis' from *Please Mrs Butler*, Kestrel Books (1983). Copyright © Allan Ahlberg 1983; and 'The Trial of Derek Drew' from *Heard it in the Playground*, Viking (1989). Copyright © Allan Ahlberg, 1989, by permission of Penguin UK; **W.H. Auden**, 'Twelve Songs XI' (Roman Wall Blues') and 'Twelve Songs IX' (Stop all the clocks') from *Collected Poems by W.H. Auden*, by permission of Faber and Faber; **Barbara Baker**, 'A Spike of Green', by permission of B. Custance Baker; **Hilaire Belloc**, 'Henry King' and 'The Tiger' from *Complete Verse*, Random House UK, by permission of The Peters Fraser and Dunlop Group Ltd on behalf of the Estate of the author; **Gerard Benson**, 'Driving Home', by permission of the author; **John Betjeman**, 'Hunter Trials' from *Collected Poems*, by permission of the estate of the author; **Laurence Binyon**, 'For the Fallen' (September 1914), by permission of The Society of Authors on behalf of the Estate of the author; **Valerie Bloom**, 'Christmas is here', 'When Granny', 'The Hyena', 'The River' and 'Water Everywhere', by permission of the author; **Dave Calder**, 'The Thirteenth day of Christmas', 'Assembly', 'Changed', 'Greengrocer' and 'Desk', by permission of the author; **Charles Causley**, 'I am the Song', 'Out in the Desert', 'Timothy Winter', 'Early in the Morning', 'All Day Saturday' and 'They're Fetching in the Holly and the Ivy' from *Collected Poems*, Macmillan, and 'Rebekah' from *Collected Poems for Children*, Macmillan, by permission of David Higham Associates on behalf of the author; **Debjani Chatterjee**, 'Proverbial Logic' first published in *Albino Gecko*, University of Salzburg Press, by permission of the author; **G.K. Chesterton**, 'Triolet', by permission of A.P. Watt Ltd on behalf of The Royal Literary Fund; **John Coldwell**, 'A Poem With Two Lauras In It', first published in *Custard Pie*, ed. Pie Corbett (1996) Macmillan, and 'Two Witches Discuss Good Grooming', by permission of the author; **Paul Cookson**, 'It's Not The Same Anymore', 'Four Crazy Pets', 'I Wish I'd Been At Christmas Past' from *Sing That Joke* by Paul Cookson (1998) Solway Publishers, ' This Year I Will Stay Awake' from *We Three Kings*, ed. Brian Moses(1998) Macmillan, and 'Where Teachers Keep Their Pets' from *Teacher's Pets* (1999) Macmillan, by permission of the author; **Wendy Cope**, 'An Attempt at Unrhymed Verse', by permission of the author; **Pie Corbett**, 'Wings' and 'A Chance in France', included in *An Odd Kettle of Fish*, Macmillan Children's Books.

Acknowledgements

Copyright © Pie Corbett, by permission of the author; **Sue Cowling**, 'Classroom Helper' included in *Teachers' Pets*, Macmillan Children's Books, by permission of the author; and 'Ten Syllables for Spring' from *What is a Kumquat?* (1991), by permission of Faber and Faber Ltd; e.e. **cummings**, 'in Just-' and 'little tree', from *Complete Poems 1904-62*, ed. George J. Firmage. Copyright © 1991 by the Trustees for the e.e. cummings Trust and George James Firmage, by permission of W.W. Norton & Company Ltd; **John Cunliffe**, 'Cat Warmth' from *Standing on a Strawberry*, Andre Deutsch, by permission of David Higham Associates on behalf of the author; W.H. Davies, 'Leisure' from *The Complete Poems*, Jonathan Cape, by permission of Random House UK on behalf of the Executors of the Estate of the author; **Jan Dean**, 'An Owl Flew into my Bedroom', by permission of the author; **Roald Dahl**, 'Little Red Riding Hood' from *Revolting Rhymes*, Jonathan Cape, by permission of David Higham Associates on behalf of the Estate of the author; **Emily Dickinson**, 'To make a prairie' (Poem 1755) and 'The moon' (Poem 737) from *The Poems of Emily Dickinson*, ed. Thomas H. Johnson, The Belknap Press of Harvard University Press. Copyright © 1951, 1955, 1979, 1983 by the President and Fellows of Harvard College, by permission of the publishers and the Trustees of Amherst College; **Peter Dixon**, 'Last Waltz', 'Down Jericho Way', 'Lost Garden' and 'A Silly Thing to Do' from *Peter Dixon's Grand Prix of Poetry*, Macmillan Children's Books, by permission of the author; **Lord Alfred Douglas**, 'The Cod', by permission of Sheila Colman, Executor of the Literary Estate of the author; **Carol Ann Duffy**, 'Lies' and 'Prior Knowledge'. Copyright © Carol Ann Duffy, by permission of the author. **Richard Edwards**, 'Sam Said' and 'Judith' from *A Mouse in My Roof*, Penguin UK, 'Just My Luck' and 'Bedtime' from *Whispers from a Wardrobe*, Penguin UK, and 'Bramble Talk', by permission of the author; **T.S. Eliot**, 'The Song of the Jellicles' and 'Skimbleshanks: The Railway Cat' from *Old Possum's Book of Practical Cats*. Copyright © 1939 by T.S. Eliot and renewed 1967 by Esme Valerie Eliot, by permission of Faber and Faber Ltd; **Eleanor Farjeon**, 'Night Will Never Stay', 'Pencil and Paint', 'Sounds in the Evening' from *Silver Sand and Snow*, Michael Joseph, 'Poppies' and 'Myfanwy Among the Leaves' from *The Children's Bells*, Oxford University Press, and 'Cottage' from *Then There Were Three*, Michael Joseph, by permission of David Higham Associates on behalf of the Estate of the author; **Max Fatchen**, 'Isn't It Amazing' and 'Just in Case' from *Peculiar Rhymes and Lunatic Lines*, by permission of Orchard Books, a division of The Watts Publishing Group Ltd; **Michael Flanders**, 'The Hippopotamus Song'. Copyright © 1952, Warner/Chappell Music Ltd, London, by permission of IMP Ltd; **Rachel Field**, 'Something Told the Wild Geese' from *Poems*, Macmillan, New York (1957), by permission of Simon & Schuster Books for Young Readers, an imprint of Simon & Schuster Children's Publishing Division; **John Foster**, 'My Baby Brother's Secrets', first published in *I'm Telling On You*, ed. Brian Moses, Macmillan. Copyright ©

Acknowledgements

1999 John Foster, by permission of the author; **Robert Frost**, 'The Blue-Butterfly Day' from *The Poetry of Robert Frost*, ed. Edward Connery Lathem, Jonathan Cape, by permission of Random House UK; **Rose Fyleman**, 'A Fairy Went A-Marketing', by permission of The Society of Authors as the Literary Representative of the Estate of the author; **Carmen de Gaszthold**, 'The Prayer of the Little Ducks' from *Prayers from the Ark*, trans. Rumer Godden, 1963, by permission of Macmillan Children's Books; **Kenneth Grahame**, 'Duck's Ditty' from *The Wind in the Willows*. Copyright © The University Chest, Oxford, by permission of Curtis Brown Ltd on behalf of The University Chest, Oxford; **Nigel Gray**, 'My Cat' by permission of the author; **David Greygoose**, 'The Farmer's Cat', after a translation by Xia Lu, by permission of the author; **Philip Gross**, 'Growler' from *All-Nite Café*, 'The Cat's Muse' from *Manifold Manor*, by permission of Faber and Faber Ltd; and 'Visiting Mrs Neverly', by permission of the author; **Mike Harding**, 'Christmas Market' from *Buns For The Elephants*, Viking, 1995. Copyright © Mike Harding 1995; **David Harmer**, 'Will It Go To a Replay?', 'Divali' and 'On a Blue Day', by permission of the author; **Ernest Henry**, 'The Song of Arabella Jellyfish' from *Poems to Shout Out Loud*, by permission of Bloomsbury Publishing; **Seamus Heaney**, 'Mid-Term Break' from *Open Ground*, by permission of Faber and Faber Ltd; **John Hegley**, 'The Emergensea' and 'Children With Adults', by permission Peters Fraser & Dunlop Group Ltd on behalf of the author; **Adrian Henri**, 'Kate's Unicorn', 'The Tomcat of Notra Dame' and 'Refugee' from *Robocat* (1998), by permission of Bloomsbury Publishing; **Russell Hoban**, 'The Friendly Cinnamon Bun', 'Small, Smaller' and 'Typo' from *The Pedalling Man*, Heinemann, by permission of David Higham Associates on behalf of the author; **A.E. Housman**, 'When I Was One and Twenty', 'Into my Heart an Air that Kills' and 'The Grizzly Bear', by permission of The Society of Authors as the literary representative of the Estate of the author; **James Hurley**, 'Greedy Dog', by permission of the author; **Ted Hughes**, 'Foxgloves' from *Moonwhales,* and 'My Father' from *Meet My Folks!*, by permission of Faber & Faber Ltd; **Elizabeth Jennings**, 'Given an Apple' from *Collected Poems*, Carcanet, by permission of David Higham Associates on behalf of the author; **Jenny Joseph**, 'The Sun has Burst the Sky', 'The Un-developers', 'Towards the end of summer' and 'November Returns' from *Selected Jenny Joseph*, Macmillan, and 'Getting Back Home', by permission of John Johnson (Literary Agent) Ltd on behalf of the author; **Mike Jubb**, 'Secret Love', by permission of the author; **Bobbi Katz**, 'Cat Kisses'. Copyright © 1974 by Bobbi Katz, renewed 1996, by permission of the author; **Jackie Kay**, 'Pomegranate', 'At Home Abroad', 'Summer Romance', 'The Frog Who Dreamed She Was an Opera Singer' and 'Grandpa's Soup' from *The Frog who dreamed she was an Opera Singer*, by permission of Bloomsbury Publishing; **Rudyard Kipling**, 'A Smuggler's Song', by permission of A.P. Watt Ltd on behalf of The National Trust for Places of Historic Interest or Natural Beauty; **James Kirkup**, 'The Kitten and the Falling Snow', by per-

Acknowledgements

mission of the author; **Karla Kuskin**, 'If You, Like Me' from *Any Me I Want to Be*. Copyright © 1972 by Karla Kuskin, by permission of Scott Treimel New York on behalf of the author; **Tony Langham**, for 'Sir's a Secret Agent', by permission of the author; **Philip Larkin**, 'The Explosion' from *Collected Poems*, by permission of Faber and Faber Ltd; **John Latham**, 'Weasels', by permission of the author; **D.H. Lawrence**, 'Self-Pity' and 'Twenty Years Ago' from *The Complete Poems of D.H. Lawrence*, ed. V. de Sola Pinto and F.W. Roberts. Copyright © 1964, 1971 by Angelo Ravagli and C.M. Weekley, Executors of the Estate of Frieda Lawrence Ravagli, by permission of Laurence Pollinger Ltd on behalf of the Estate of Frieda Lawrence Ravagli; **Dennis Lee**, 'Silverly', from *Garbage Delight* (1977) Macmillan of Canada. Copyright © 1977 Dennis Lee, by permission of Westwood Creative Artists on behalf of the author; **C.S. Lewis**, 'The Late Passenger' from *Narrative Poems*, by permission of HarperCollins Publishers Ltd; **Shelagh McGee**, 'Wanted: A Witch's Cat', by permission of the author; **Roger McGough**, 'MARCH ingorders', 'The Leader', 'Sky in the Pie' and 'Snow and Ice Poems' from *Sky in the Pie*, Viking Kestrel, 'Cousin Nell', 'The Writer of this Poem' and 'Slug', by permission of Peters Fraser and Dunlop Group Ltd on behalf of the author; **Ian McMillan**, 'No Bread', 'Spot the Hidden Part of a Loaf', 'School in the Holidays', 'The Dragon's Birthday Party', 'Ready Salted' and 'Out of Season'; and 'No Points' by Ian and Andrew Macmillan, by permission of the author; **Colin McNaughton**, 'Potty' from *Who's Been Sleeping in My Porridge?* Copyright © 1990 Colin McNaughton, by permission of Walker Books Ltd; **Lindsay MacRae**, 'Animal Rights' from *You Canny Shove Your Granny Off a Bus*, Viking, 1995. Copyright © Lindsay MacRae 1995, by permission of The Agency (London) Ltd on behalf of the author; **Wes Magee**, 'The Tunneller' from *Lost Property Box*, Macmillan, by permission of the author; **Walter de la Mare**, 'Hide and Seek', 'The Bookworm' and 'Someone' from *The Complete Poems of Walter de la Mare*, 1969, by permission of the Literary Trustees of the author and The Society of Authors as their representative; **Linda Marshall**, 'Close Cropped Hair' included in *Unzip Your Lips Again*, ed. Paul Cookson, by permission of the author; **Gerda Mayer**, 'Shallow Poem' from *Bernini's Cat* (1999) Iron Press, first published in *Ambit* (1971) . Copyright © Gerda Mayer, by permission of the author; **Robin Mellor**, 'Nursery Rhyme', by permission of the author; **Eve Merriam**, 'Fantasia' and 'Thumbprint' from *A Sky Full of Poems* by Eve Merriam. Copyright © 1964, 1970, 1973 by Eve Merriam, by permission of Marian Reiner on behalf of the Estate of the author; **Spike Milligan**, 'Teeth', 'Rain' and 'You Must Never Bath in an Irish Stew', by permission of Spike Milligan Productions Ltd; **Trevor Millum**, 'The Dark Avenger', first published in *Double Talk* by Trevor Milum and Bernard Young, by permission of the author; **A.A. Milne**, 'Happiness' from *When We Were Very Young*', Methuen Children's Books. Copyright © A.A. Milne; 'Us Two' and 'Furry Bear' from *Now We Are Six*, Methuen Children's Books. Copyright © A.A.

Acknowledgements

Milne, by permission of Egmont Children's Books Ltd; **Adrian Mitchell**, 'Nobody Rides the Unicorn'. Copyright © Adrian Mitchell, by permission of The Peters Fraser and Dunlop Group Ltd on behalf of the author; **Tony Mitton**, 'Salestalk' from *Tongue Twisters & Tonsil Twizzlers* (1997) Macmillan. Copyright © Tony Mitton 1997, by permission of David Higham Associates on behalf of the author; **John Mole**, 'The Goldfish' from *The Mad Parrots Countdown*, and 'The Invisible Man', by permission of the author; **Edwin Morgan**, 'The Computer's First Christmas Card' from *Collected Poems*, by permission of Carcanet Press Ltd; **Brian Morse**, 'James Had a Magic Set for Christmas' from *Picnic on the Moon* (1990), by permission of Turton & Chambers Ltd; **Brian Moses**, 'The Lost Angels' and 'The Bonfire at Barton Point' from *Don't Look at Me in That Tone of Voice*, Penguin, by permission of the author; **Frances Nagle**, 'Dream Team' from *You can't call a hedgehog Hopscotch*, Dagger Press, by permission of the author; **Ogden Nash**, 'The Eel' and 'Good Riddance but Now What?' from *Candy is Dandy: The Best of Ogden Nash*, by permission of Andre Deutsch Ltd; **Judith Nicholls**, 'Magic' from *Dragonsfire*, Faber & Faber. Copyright © 1990 Judith Nichols; 'Spring Magic' and an extract from 'Five Answers to the Question – Where did Winter Go?'. Copyright © 1999 Judith Nicholls, by permission of the author; **Grace Nichols**, 'For Forest' from *Come On Into My Tropical Garden* (1988) A & C Black, and 'Conkers', both included in *Lazy Thoughts of a Lazy Woman* (1989) Virago; 'When My Friend Anita Runs' from *Give Yourself a Hug* (1994) A & C Black; and 'My Parakeet' from *No Hickory No Dickory No Dock*. Copyright © Grace Nichols 1988, 1989, 1991, 1994, by permission of Curtis Brown Ltd on behalf of the author; **Alfred Noyes**, 'The Highwayman' from *Collected Poems*, by permission of John Murray (Publishers) Ltd; **David Orme**, 'Town Dog', by permission of the author; **Gareth Owen**, 'Bird' from *The Fox on the Roundabout* (1995) Young Lions, 'Typewriting Class' from *Song of the City* (1985) HarperCollins, and 'Saturdays' and 'The Wind' from *Salford Road* (1988) Young Lions; and 'Shell' (1999). Copyright © Gareth Owen 1985, 1988,1995, 1999, by permission of Rogers, Coleridge & White Ltd on behalf of the author; **Brian Patten**, 'Grumbly Moon', 'Rabbit's Spring', 'Small Wonders' and 'The Pet Wig' from *Thawing Frozen Frogs* (1990) Viking. Copyright © Brian Patten 1990; and 'You'd Better Believe Him' from *Notes to the Hurrying Man* (1980) Allen & Unwin. Copyright © Brian Patten 1969, by permission of Rogers, Coleridge and White on behalf of the author; and 'The Vampire Duck' by permission of the author; **Kenneth Patchen**, 'The Magical Mouse' from *The Collected Poems of Kenneth Patchen*. Copyright © 1957 by New Directions Publishing Corp., by permission of New Directions Publishing Corp.; **Noel Petty**, 'What For!' from *This Poem Doesn't Rhyme*, ed. Gerard Benson, Puffin Books, by permission of Campbell Thomson & McLaughlin Ltd on behalf of the author; **Gervase Phinn**, 'Class Discussion', by permission of the author; **Christopher Pilling**, 'The Meeting Place' from *Poems for*

Christmas, 1982, by permission of Peterloo Poets; **Jack Prelutsky**, 'Nine Mice' from *New Kid on the Block*, Heinemann Young Books. Copyright © Jack Prelutsky 1984, by permission of Egmont Children's Books Ltd; **John Pudney**, 'For Johnny' from *Collected Poems*, J.M. Dent, by permission of David Higham Associates on behalf of the author; **Irene Rawnsley**, 'Woolly Mammoth' (1990), by permission of the author; **James Reeves**, 'The Old Wife and the Ghost' from *Complete Poems for Children*, Heinemann. Copyright © James Reeves, by permission of Laura Cecil Literary Agency on behalf of the Estate of the author; **John Rice**, 'Instructions for Giants' and 'Ghost', by permission of the author; **E.V. Rieu**, 'The Hippopotamus's Birthday', by permission of Authors' Licensing Collecting Society on behalf of the Estate of the author; **Michael Rosen**, 'Talking Tubes' and 'Mr Baggs' from *You Wait Till I'm Older*, Viking; and 'I Know Someone Who Can', by permission of The Peters Fraser and Dunlop Group Ltd on behalf of the author; **Andrew Rumsey**, 'Secret Affair', by permission of the author; **Siegfried Sassoon**, 'Everyone Sang', by permission of Barbara Levy Literary Agency on behalf of George Sassoon; **Vernon Scannell**, 'The Day that Summer Died', 'Jason's Trial', 'The Apple Raid', 'Love Light' and 'Epitaph for a Gifted Man', by permission of the author; **Fred Sedgwick**, 'Cinquain – Prayer, February Night', by permission of the author; **Andrea Shavick**, 'Auntie Betty Thinks She's Batgirl', by permission of the author; **Shel Silverstein**, 'Minnow Minnie' from *Where the Sidewalk Ends*. Copyright © 1974 by Evil Eye Music, Inc; and 'Sun Hat' from *Falling Up*. Copyright © 1996 by Evil Eye Music, Inc, by permission of Edite Kroll Literary Agency, Inc on behalf of the estate of the author; **Matt Simpson**, 'Rhinoceros' and 'A Dog's Life' from *The Pigs' Thermal Underwear* (1993) Headland Publications, by permission of the estate of the author; **Stevie Smith**, 'Cat Asks Mouse Out' and 'Not Waving but Drowning' from *The Collected Poems of Stevie Smith*, Penguin, by permission of James MacGibbon; **Roger Stevens**, 'Mobile Home for Sale', by permission of the author; **Matthew Sweeney**, 'In the Desert', by permission of the author; **Marian Swinger**, 'The First Christmas', by permission of the author; **Dylan Thomas**, 'Fern Hill' from *Collected Poems*, J.M. Dent, by permission of David Higham Associates on behalf of the Estate of the author; **Nick Toczek**, 'Problems in the School of Fish', by permission of the author; **Barry Turrell**, 'Lauren' from *Inky Foot 1993*, by permission of WH Smith Group PLC; **William Carlos Williams**, 'This is Just to Say' from *Collected Poems*, by permission of Carcanet Press Ltd; **Raymond Wilson**, 'Never Since Eden', by permission of G.M. Wilson; **Judith Wright**, 'Legend' from *A Human Pattern: Selected Poems* (1995), by permission of ETT Imprint, Sydney; **Kit Wright**, 'March Dusk', 'Applause' and 'Just Before Christmas', by permission of the author; **W.B. Yeats**, 'The Song of the Wandering Aengus', 'The Lake Isle of Innisfree' and 'When You Are Old' from *The Collected Poems of W.B. Yeats*, revised and edited by Richard J. Finneran, by permission of A.P. Watt on behalf of Michael Yeats; **Andrew Young**, 'Late Autumn' from *Selected*

Acknowledgements

Poems, by permission of Carcanet Press Ltd; **Benjamin Zephaniah**, 'Heroes' and 'Body Talk' from *Talking Turkeys* by Benjamin Zephaniah (1994) Viking. Copyright © Benjamin Zephaniah, 1994, by permission of Penguin UK.

Every effort has been made to trace the copyright holders but if any have been inadvertently overlooked the publishers will be pleased to make the necessary arrangement at the first opportunity.